DANCING IN THE STORM

AMIE DARNELL SPECHT
and SHANNON HITCHCOCK

 ROCKY POND BOOKS

ROCKY POND BOOKS

An imprint of Penguin Random House LLC, New York

First published in the United States of America by Rocky Pond Books,
an imprint of Penguin Random House LLC, 2024

Rocky Pond Books is a registered trademark and the colophon
is a trademark of Penguin Random House LLC.

The Penguin colophon is a registered trademark
of Penguin Books Limited.

Visit us online at PenguinRandomHouse.com.

Library of Congress Cataloging-in-Publication Data is available.

1st Printing

Printed in the United States of America

LSCH • Design by Jason Henry • Text set in Marselis Serif Pro

For Dr. Frederick S. Kaplan,
who has devoted his life to unraveling the mysteries of FOP,
and for all those affected by it—past, present, and future.

Table of Contents

A JUMPING BEAN

I wanted to be a champion.

At gymnastics competitions, floor was my favorite event—a chance to dance and tumble to music. This time my parents and my brother, Chris, were in the stands, and my grandparents were watching too. They had planned their visit from West Virginia to Baton Rouge around my meet. I wanted to make them proud, especially Grandma. When I was seven and she first saw me somersaulting on Chris's trampoline, she'd said, "Sign Kate up for gymnastics. She reminds me of Mary Lou Retton—a regular jumping bean." Mary Lou had competed a long time ago, but since she grew up in West Virginia, she's a hometown hero.

I saluted the judges, blocking out the girls who were competing at the same time on vault, bars, and beam.

When the music started, a burst of adrenaline shot through me. I dropped to my knees, then sprang up and danced across the floor. I took off running and vaulted into a roundoff, back handspring, back layout.

Hamming it up, I snapped my fingers to the theme from *The Addams Family*. My confidence soared as people in the crowd snapped their fingers too.

I strutted and posed, completed an aerial and another tumbling pass. Spinning around, I danced across the floor for my grand finale. I picked up speed, jumped into a front tuck, and stepped out into a front handspring. A big smile spread across my face as I chasséd into my final pose.

The music stopped and I raised my arms to salute the judges. My teammates cheered, but Grandpa was louder. "Way to go, Bean! Mary Lou's got nothing on you!"

The gymnast who performed after me stepped out of bounds—an automatic deduction. Three more girls competed after her. I imagined my picture hanging beside the one of Mary Lou in Frank's Place, a restaurant near my grandparents' house.

"They're posting final results," Coach whispered.

My teeth and fists clenched.

I . . . I couldn't believe it!

Coach B. pounced on me like a cat. "You did it! Congratulations, Kate. You took the gold!"

"I . . . I really did?" I'd been in this position before and never won.

"Don't look so surprised! I always knew you'd be a champion."

I gazed into the stands. Grandma and Grandpa hugged. Mom, Dad, and Chris cheered. They were proud of me. I pumped my fist in the air.

It would have been a perfect moment, except with every pump of my fist, my shoulder throbbed.

CRAWFISH BOIL

I wanted the last day of my grandparents' visit to be perfect. Grandma and I sat at the kitchen table with our *Really Relaxing Colouring Books*. I had *Gorgeous Geometrics*, and she had *Botanicals in Bloom*.

"I miss you already," Grandma said, "but it's not long until Christmas."

Memories of West Virginia gave me a wistful feeling: snowy mountain peaks, sledding, mugs of hot chocolate. "Christmas is still three months away. I wish we lived closer."

"West Virginia is home, but there are lots of good things about living in Baton Rouge too," Grandma said.

I colored a rectangle and thought of hot beignets

topped with powdered sugar, LSU football games, Mardi Gras parades, and courtyards filled with flowers. But the best thing about Baton Rouge was that my two best friends lived close by.

"You're frowning," Grandma said. "What are you thinking about?"

I didn't tell her my left shoulder felt tight. Aches and pains were just part of being a gymnast. "Claire and Mindy."

"Such nice girls," Grandma said. "And I loved meeting their families."

Claire's and Mindy's families couldn't have been more different. Claire's dad was a lawyer. Her mom did a lot of volunteer work and ran our Girl Scout troop. Mindy's dad left when she was a baby, which meant her mom had to work two jobs and didn't have much time for volunteering.

Grandma held up the picture she'd colored of red roses and yellow daylilies. "While you finish, I'm going to see about helping your mom with dinner."

"Oh, I think she's napping. Dad's cooking tonight."

"Mmmm," Grandma said. "Something sure smells good."

"Babka. Dad's making my favorite dessert!"

*   *   *

To give Grandma and Grandpa a real Louisiana send-off, we had a crawfish boil. Dad filled a large pot with five gallons of water and added his secret spice blend. He set the kitchen timer for forty minutes, waiting on the spices to work their magic. "Bean," he said, "how about keeping an eye on the water? After golfing in the hot sun, I could use a shower."

"Sure," I said. I played around on my phone, trying to ignore my shoulder, while I waited for the water to boil. Dad returned just in time to add the potatoes, corn, garlic, and andouille sausage. He covered the pot. "Won't be long now," he said. "Almost time for the crawfish."

A crawfish boil was one of my favorite things about living in Baton Rouge. We always ate them outside on a table covered with newspapers.

At the end of dinner, Grandpa held his water glass in the air. "It's been a perfect visit. A toast to Kate and her gold medal!"

"And a toast to Chris and his solo in show choir," Grandma added. "I'm so proud of both of you!"

Chris blushed. He was an introvert who loved to play video games, but he had this amazing voice. It was almost like he became a different person when he sang.

I looked around the table, lingering on each member of my family. Mom was an only child. My grandparents loved her so much she couldn't help but pass it on to Chris and me. I wasn't just Bean, but *Lucky Bean* when it came to families, and Grandpa said they'd had a perfect visit.

Mission accomplished.

HELLO, EARTHLINGS

I wanted to have a friend over, but first I had to help Mom clean the guest room. I took a deep breath, inhaling the scent of Grandpa's Mennen aftershave lotion. The minty smell always lingered and made me miss him even more.

"Cheer up," Mom said, stretching a fitted sheet across the bed. "Before you know it, Grandma will be sending us fudge and Chex Mix for Christmas."

My eyes filled with tears. It wasn't just my grandparents. My shoulder ached a lot.

"Hey, what's wrong?" Mom said. She dropped the pillow on the bed and walked over to give me a hug.

"Grandma and Grandpa . . . and . . . and Chloe," I

sobbed. My dog, Chloe, had died last spring. I didn't want to tell Mom about my shoulder, and so I pretended I was crying about Chloe.

"Ah, Bean. Maybe it's time for another dog."

"No! Another dog could never replace Chloe."

"Of course not, but your heart has room for another pet. Just think about it."

Mom was crazy about dogs. Animals of all kinds, really. It's why she worked in a vet's office. "Could . . . could I invite Mindy or Claire for a sleepover?"

She rubbed my back in slow circles. "Your muscles are tight. You must have been practicing too hard. Why don't you invite them both?"

"Because last time wasn't much fun. All Claire wanted to do was show off her tumbling skills, and Mindy's not into gymnastics."

"Hmmm. If I were only going to invite one of them, I'd pick the one I have the most fun with."

This was my mom's superpower: She hardly ever told me what to do, but she usually nudged me in the right direction.

Dad grilled hamburgers for dinner and then set up his telescope for Mindy and me. We had first become friends at space camp in Huntsville, Alabama. If I had

9

a sister, I'd want her to be just like Mindy. We sort of looked alike—same long brown hair and hazel eyes, but Mindy had freckles across the bridge of her nose and wore glasses.

Mindy was the kind of friend who cheered the loudest when I won a gymnastics medal. She had read Simone Biles's autobiography because I did, even though she wasn't interested in gymnastics. Gazing at the stars was Mindy's favorite thing to do at my house because she wanted to be an astronaut.

Mindy and I spread a blanket on the ground. I tried lying on my back, but the pressure made my shoulder blade throb.

"Look at those stars and planets," Mindy said reverently. She pointed with her index finger. "There's Venus."

Mindy had a cute face, but when she studied the night sky, instead of cute, her excitement made her beautiful. It didn't seem fair that we had a telescope and somebody who loved space as much as Mindy didn't. "Go ahead. You can use it first."

Once I had cluelessly told Mindy she should buy a telescope of her own. She had gotten very still and quiet. "Kate, I went to space camp on a scholarship. We don't have the extra money for a telescope."

After that I started paying more attention. Mindy's mom was a secretary, and then worked in a fabric store on the weekends. Their house was smaller than ours, the paint was peeling, and their furniture was really old. Mindy and I went to different schools, and just like her neighborhood wasn't as nice as ours, neither was her school. Our parent-teacher organization paid for extra stuff, like new gym equipment.

Mindy adjusted the telescope's lens while I played the music from *Hamilton* on my phone. Broadway musicals were a favorite of mine.

I slapped at a mosquito on my ankle. "Hurry up. The mosquitoes are eating me alive."

"Five more minutes," Mindy begged.

I took a turn looking at Venus through the telescope, but my mind was on dessert. "Want to make a sheet cake?"

"Yes," Mindy said, "after I have one more look through the telescope."

Chris came home from his friend Izaak's house and stuck his head in the kitchen. "Hello, earthlings."

He and Mindy had called each other earthlings ever since space camp. "What are you baking?" he asked. "Can I have some?"

Mindy explained how most people use frosting out of a can, but not us. We were scientists in the middle of an experiment—our task was to make rainbow chip icing by using melted white chocolate and food coloring.

Chris watched, and soon we had four small bowls of melted chocolate: one colored blue, one yellow, one pink, and one green.

"What's next?" he asked.

"We have to spread the colors on parchment paper and refrigerate them," I said. "After they harden, we'll dice them into chips."

Mindy had food coloring on her hands and turned on the faucet to wash it off. "And while the chips are cooling, we'll make vanilla frosting," she added.

Chris studied the recipe we'd printed from the Sally's Baking Addiction website. "You girls are lucky I'm here," he announced. "I'll read you the instructions while you work."

I rolled my eyes at him. "You just want to help eat the cake."

"That too," he admitted.

Sometimes I gave Chris a hard time, but he always had my back. Once when we were little, a mean kid had put soap in his water gun and squirted me in the face.

I cried because the soap stung my eyes. Chris pounced on that kid like a professional wrestler. Yep, Chris was all right as far as brothers went, and though neither earthling would ever admit it, I was pretty sure he and Mindy had a crush on each other.

FIVE OAKS MIDDLE SCHOOL

Chris's friend Izaak Jackson had a locker right beside mine. "What's up, Bean? Bring home the gold at your gymnastics meet?"

I hadn't been thinking about gymnastics, but about Girl Scouts. I needed to decide what badge I wanted to work on next. "Yes! I finally won gold, and I have the sore shoulder to prove it."

"Probably headed to the Olympics," he said.

My face heated up. Izaak was cute, and now he was complimenting me.

But he was also full of baloney. When we had first moved to Baton Rouge, I'd asked him if he'd ever seen an alligator.

"Seen one?" he'd said, puffing his chest out. "My dad *hunts* alligators. He's the Steve Irwin of Louisiana."

Bindi Irwin's dad, Steve, used to host a TV show called *The Crocodile Hunter.* "Really?" I'd asked, impressed.

Izaak had slapped his thigh as a big smile snuck across his face. "Nah, I was just messing with you. He works downtown in the mayor's office."

"You and Chris ready for our algebra test?" he asked.

"I'm ready, but Chris is probably sweating it," I said.

Izaak grinned. "That boy's still mad you were smart enough to skip fifth grade."

We were all in seventh grade even though I was a year younger.

On the way to algebra, I asked, "Did your mom bake chocolate chip cookies this weekend?"

"Of course. She's the queen of chocolate chip cookies."

"My dad baked babka." I knew it was one of Izaak's favorites. "Want to trade?"

"I would trade my trumpet for babka," he said.

I usually had lunch with the girls on my gymnastics team: Claire, Natalie, and Izaak's twin sister, Jayla. I thought of them as my second family.

"What'd you girls do over the weekend?" Claire asked.

"Visited family in N'Orleans," Jayla said. She rolled the two words into one the way people from Louisiana usually did.

"I had to babysit my brother," Nat said. "We built a city out of Legos."

"I haven't built anything with Legos in a long time," I said. "That sounds like fun. We had a crawfish boil with my grandparents, and after they left, Mindy slept over."

"Oh . . . I wondered why I didn't hear from you," Claire said. "I should have known you were hanging out with the space cadet." She laughed like she was kidding, but I knew better. Since Mindy wasn't on our gymnastics team or in Girl Scouts, Claire didn't have much time for her.

"How was *your* weekend?" I asked.

"Great! I spent Saturday morning in the gym working on my bars routine, and then we had Coach Buchanan over for dinner. She gave me some pointers on how to stick my landings. I bet none of the rest of you even *practiced* your gymnastics routines."

Jayla narrowed her eyes. "I told you we were out of town."

16

Nat shrugged, then took a bite out of her turkey sandwich.

While Claire launched into a motivational speech on winning districts and placing at States, I looked down at my salad. I loved gymnastics, I really did. But I also wanted to look through the telescope, watch *Say Yes to the Dress*, and bake with Mindy. Claire never understood about balance—unless it involved the balance beam.

I unwrapped squares of the rainbow chip frosted cake I'd brought for my friends. "Hey, Claire, what's your mom got planned for Girl Scouts on Wednesday?"

Jayla turned and whispered to me. "Good move. Way to change the subject."

Our Girl Scout meetings were always on Wednesday nights because we had gymnastics practice on Monday, Tuesday, Thursday, and Fridays. I was hoping the day off would give my shoulder time to heal.

Mom parked in front of Jayla and Izaak's house. It had a trellis with climbing roses and a wraparound porch. "Text me when you're ready to be picked up."

Izaak answered the door. "Beanie Weenie, you're late. Mrs. Chevalier was about to start without you."

"Sorry. Mom was running behind at work and we didn't eat dinner on time."

"Girls have taken over the house," Izaak muttered. "I've been banished to the basement."

I followed him to the kitchen and den that flowed together into one large room. Jayla sat at one of the card tables drawing a picture of the LSU tiger mascot. The other girls were talking and writing in their journals.

Mrs. Chevalier clapped her hands to get our attention. "Now that Kate's here, we'll start the meeting by saying the *Girl Scout Promise and Law.*"

I had memorized both of them. My favorite part was the ending: *Make the world a better place, and be a sister to every Girl Scout.* I was a good sister, but I wasn't sure how to make the world a better place. I had been wondering a lot about it, though, ever since I'd joined the troop.

Mrs. Chevalier handed out copies of the requirements for the Cadette badges. "We'll use tonight as a planning session. Read through the PDFs and choose a badge you want to work toward between now and Christmas."

I picked up the Woodworker printout because it reminded me of Grandpa. He had a workshop behind his house that was full of tools. Once I'd counted all the hammers—there were twenty of them. When my mom was growing up, she'd helped Grandpa in his workshop. She'd even made a hope chest that was still in my parents' bedroom.

Nat pushed her short brown hair off her forehead. "I want to go for the Trailblazing or Field Day badge. Something outdoors."

"Not me," Jayla said, wrinkling her nose. "I want to earn the Book Artist badge." She pointed to one of the requirements. "Look! I could visit a real art studio and interview an illustrator."

I put the Woodworker PDF back on the table, then picked up the Animal Helpers badge info. The beginning said, *Explore the connection between animals and humans.* I knew all about being connected to an animal because of Chloe.

"I know exactly which badge I want to earn next," Claire said. "Financing My Dreams. I'll get to explore dream jobs, price my dream home, research dream vacations..."

Claire was good at dreaming big, and most of the time I admired that about her. I read through the Night Owl PDF because it reminded me of Mindy. She would love exploring nature at night.

"Here," Claire said. She took the Night Owl packet out of my hand and pushed the Public Speaker one in front of me. "You should work on this one."

I didn't want to consider it because Claire had been so bossy, but I loved reading aloud in class. I enjoyed singing along to Broadway musicals. I sometimes acted out movie parts in front of my bedroom mirror. I read the requirements. *Write a speech about something you believe in.* I'd never really thought about what I believed in, but the Public Speaker badge was more interesting than all the others combined. It fit me perfectly.

MAKING MINDY HAPPY

After Girl Scouts, I turned on the backyard lights and jumped for a while on Chris's trampoline. It felt different, more peaceful, bouncing under the stars than with the sun beating down. Baton Rouge was hot and muggy, even in the fall.

I thought of Mindy as I tumbled and flipped. She would love working on the Night Owl badge, but so far, I hadn't been able to convince her to join Girl Scouts. The last time I mentioned it, we'd both ended up feeling sad.

"Kate, my mom works two jobs," she'd said. "When I get home from school, instead of gymnastics or Girl

Scouts, I have a list of chores, and then I start dinner."

"But we only meet once a week, and we take great field trips."

"Field trips cost money," Mindy said. "It makes a big difference when you only have one parent working."

"I guess."

"It's true," Mindy insisted. "Your dad's an engineer. Engineers make a lot more money than admins. It's why Mom is so strict about my grades. She expects me to get a scholarship and go to college."

Mindy studied a lot more than I did. As I completed a couple of backflips, I thought about the poster of Sally Ride, the first American woman in space, that hung in Mindy's bedroom. Her birthday was coming up, and I had found the perfect gift at a yard sale. It's funny how people buy expensive items, only use them a time or two, and then sell them cheap. I'd gotten a real bargain.

"Bean," Mom yelled. "Get off that trampoline and head for the shower. You're bound to smell worse than a West Virginia polecat."

"What's a polecat?" I asked, but Mom didn't hear me.

I hurried inside. After my shower, I stood wrapped

in a towel, staring at my back in the bathroom mir-ror. It *looked* normal but had been tight and achy ever since my last gymnastics meet.

Chris knocked on the door. "Hey, have you turned into a mermaid in there? I need a shower too."

"Just a sec." I quickly pulled on my shorty pajamas and hung up my towel. "The bathroom is all yours, big brother. I'm going to call Mindy."

"Oh, tell her I said . . . tell her I said . . . hi."

"How original," I teased. "She'll be really im-pressed."

I left Chris and plopped down on my bed. My room was nothing like Mindy's. Instead of astronauts, I had posters of my favorite gymnasts on the walls—Aly Raisman, Simone Biles, and Gabby Douglas.

I reached for my phone and called Mindy.

"How was Girl Scouts?" she asked.

I sighed. "Claire was bossy, but as usual, she had a great idea." I told Mindy about the badges we all planned to work on.

"Here's what I think about Claire," Mindy said. "Mrs. Chevalier pushes her to be perfect, and then Claire pushes you and the rest of her friends the same way."

"That's no excuse. I hate being bossed around."

"She was right, though," Mindy said. "You're a good public speaker. I've thought so ever since you played Tinkerbell in *Peter Pan*."

Peter Pan had been a lot of fun. Nat had played Peter, and as Tinkerbell, I'd been hooked to wires that hung from the ceiling. I had loved flying through the air. "Hey, I was thinking about you while I was jumping on the trampoline. I know what you told me about not having time for Girl Scouts, but I did some research. You could be an individually registered Girl Scout. You wouldn't have to attend troop meetings and could work at your own pace. There's a Night Owl badge that has virtual field trips."

"What kind of virtual field trips?"

"Well, one of them was an observatory planetarium."

"Aaaah," Mindy squealed. "Really? Are you sure?"

"I'm positive. Google it and read about it for yourself."

"I will," Mindy said. "Just as soon as we hang up. And Kate, you're the best friend I've ever had. Thanks."

Mindy always made me feel important. A warm gooeyness spread through my chest, like Grandma's mac and cheese straight from the oven. "You're my best friend too. That's why I want us both to be Girl Scouts."

"Are we having a sleepover Saturday night?" Mindy asked. "We could talk more about it then."

"Sounds good to me, but I need to check with Mom."

I flexed my sore shoulder and winced.

NIGHT OWLS

Mom agreed that Mindy could sleep over on Saturday. Most kids would pop a frozen pizza in the oven, or call Domino's, but not Mindy and me. We made our own pizzas, even the dough.

"Did your mom buy the flour?" Mindy asked.

I stood on my tiptoes, reaching for the Anna Napoletana extra-fine flour. Mindy had researched ingredients and this one made superior pizza crusts.

While I gathered everything else we needed, Mindy read through the instructions for a second time. "It makes three pizza crusts, so there should be plenty for your parents and Chris too."

I noticed the way Mindy's cheeks flushed when she

mentioned Chris. "Don't forget Izaak. He and Chris are planning a *Star Wars* marathon."

"*Luke, I am your father,*" Mindy said in a deep voice.

Her Darth Vader imitation was spot-on. It almost made me forget my shoulder. Almost. "Hey, want to listen to music while we work?"

"Sure," Mindy said. "Since Chris . . . I mean *you* love musicals, how about *Oklahoma!*?"

Mindy played "I'm Just a Girl Who Can't Say No." The character, Ado Annie, made kissing funny. In the new version, she was played by Ali Stroker, the first actress in a wheelchair to ever win a Tony Award. It was the one thing I liked better about the new version.

After Mindy and I let the dough rise, we stretched it across the pizza pans. Great pies need fresh ingredients. We added hand-crushed tomatoes, mozzarella slices, grated Pecorino Romano cheese, and torn basil leaves.

As the yeasty smell filled the kitchen, Chris walked in, belting out "Oh What a Beautiful Morning." Izaak was right behind him.

"Anything I can do to help?" he asked Mom.

She looked up from chopping veggies for a salad, then smiled at him. "How about filling the water glasses?"

Dad caught my eye and winked. We both thought it was funny the way Izaak always charmed Mom with his good manners.

While Mindy and I served, the others gathered around the table.

"This pizza is awesome," Chris said. "Except for being a bathroom hog, you're a pretty good sister."

"Mindy, how's band practice going?" Mom asked.

"Good. I moved up to first chair flautist."

"I play the trumpet," Izaak said. "You like jazz?"

"Of course," Mindy said. "How could you be from Louisiana and not like jazz?"

What Mindy didn't realize was that she liked jazz, but Izaak *loved* it. He could talk jazz for hours and make it so entertaining, you couldn't help but hang on his every word.

"Ever heard of Buddy Bolden?" Izaak asked. "He's the king of jazz."

Mindy shook her head.

"How about King Oliver?"

Mindy shook her head again.

"He taught Louis Armstrong," Izaak said. "I've read about all the jazz greats and listened to the ones that left recordings. It's a hobby of mine."

"What are you kids up to after dinner?" Dad asked.

"Mindy joined Girl Scouts and we're going to work on her Night Owl badge," I said. "We're walking through the neighborhood with a flashlight to record night sounds and check out animals that lurk after dark."

"Sounds like you should have an adult with you for that," Mom said.

I wrinkled my nose. "Couldn't Chris and Izaak go with us instead?"

Chris kicked me under the table.

Izaak wouldn't look at me.

"Kate," Dad said, and then paused long enough to make me squirm. "I . . . I promised Izaak's parents he wouldn't leave our property after dark."

"But why?"

"Well," Dad said, "they're worried about his safety."

"Oh . . ." I appreciated that Dad was straightforward and honest with us, but my face heated up. "I'm sorry, Izaak. I wasn't thinking."

"It's not your fault," he said.

But it was my fault, even though it wasn't intentional. I didn't enjoy the rest of the meal. I couldn't stop thinking about whether or not a Black boy was truly safe in my neighborhood. Would a neighbor think he didn't belong and call the police?

After we cleared the table, Mindy and I decided to record the crickets chirping in our backyard. "That was awkward," she whispered.

"Yeah, I was embarrassed. I should have thought before I opened my big mouth."

"It never even occurred to me," Mindy said. "Izaak's family has more money than mine, so I'd always thought they were lucky."

"My grandma says there are some problems money can't fix."

I could feel Mindy staring at me through the inky darkness. "Kate, that might be true, but you shouldn't say it to somebody whose family has a lot less of it than yours does."

"Oh . . . oh . . ." I was close to tears. First I'd messed up with Izaak, and now Mindy. "I'm really sorry. I didn't mean to sound like a jerk."

Mindy shrugged.

I had never heard of any crime on our street, but still Izaak's parents were afraid. It didn't matter to me that Mindy's family didn't have much money, but since she always pointed out the differences, I had started paying more attention. I didn't want to hurt her feelings, or Izaak's either.

Sometimes it's hard to be friends with people who are not like you. I hoped Mindy and Izaak would feel it was worth it, though.

MY NEMESIS

The uneven bars were my nemesis. I stood in front of the low bar taking deep breaths. If I wanted to win an all-around title, my routine had to flow smoothly, and I had to stick my dismount. I knew what to do, but when it came to the bars, my brain and body didn't communicate very well.

Claire walked up beside me. "It's only practice, not a real meet. I don't know why you let the bars psych you out."

Technically, it wasn't all my fault. I was built short and powerful. Taller, leaner girls like Claire had an advantage on bars because their skills had a more graceful line that the judges gave high marks for.

I adjusted the straps of my grips and rubbed chalk on them. I wished my hands were bigger to make my catch-and-release moves easier.

"Close your eyes and visualize your routine," Claire instructed. "That's what I always do."

Why did she always have to be such a know-it-all? That's what I wondered, but I didn't dare say it out loud.

I rolled my shoulders to loosen up. After our next meet, I was going to tell Mom I needed physical therapy. I'd tell her sooner, but I was afraid a doctor would say I shouldn't compete.

Somehow, I managed to tune Claire out. I went over every skill in my mind, picturing myself winning another gold medal.

"You can do it," Coach Buchanan whispered. She would be spotting me—there to catch me if I fell.

I squatted onto the low bar, then jumped to the high one. Every bit of energy, every speck of concentration was focused on one thing—nailing my routine. Kips, castaways, handstands—every skill flowed smoothly into the next one. As I somersaulted through the air, I already knew I was going to stick my dismount. I could just tell!

Coach Buchanan whistled, and then shouted, "Way

to go, Kate! That's the best bars routine I've ever seen from you!"

I was so proud of myself that I was shaking. I had finally conquered the bars! I looked around for Claire to admit she'd been right, but she had disappeared. I wondered why. Was it because I'd completed a bars routine every bit as good as hers?

One thing I knew for sure: There is more than one kind of nemesis.

AN APRICOT

A hot, searing pain woke me from a sound sleep.
"Mom," I screamed. "Mom!"

Within seconds, light flooded my room, and Mom
hurried toward me in her nightgown. "Bean, what's
wrong? You're scaring me."

"My back!" I whimpered. "Must have hurt it in gymnastics."

"Take a deep breath," she said. "It's going to be all
right."

My back still throbbed, but Mom's presence soothed
me.

Gritting my teeth against the pain, I focused on
Mom's voice. *Everything will be okay. Everything will*

be okay. She helped me turn onto my right side, then pulled up my pajama top to take a look.

"Ah," she gasped.

"Mom? What's wrong?"

She lightly ran her fingers across my back. "I'm sure it's nothing to be alarmed about, but you have a lump about the size of an apricot on your shoulder blade. It's hard and hot to the touch."

"But I have a gymnastics meet tomorrow!"

Mom covered me with a light blanket, then patted my cheek. "Bean, I'm sorry, but I don't see any way you can compete."

"But I finally nailed my bars routine!"

"I'm sorry," Mom repeated, "but as soon as it's daylight, I'm calling your pediatrician."

I sobbed because it was so unfair. Mom held me tight and whispered, "Cry it out, Bean. This whole thing stinks."

It was a short drive to the pediatrician's office. Two other kids were in the waiting room with us—a toddler who couldn't sit still and a teenaged girl on crutches. I leaned against Mom, remembering other doctors' appointments. Chris had allergies, so we'd spent a lot of time here. I'd never had a lump before, but in Simone

Biles's autobiography, she wrote about having a bone spur. Maybe I had one of those.

"We're lucky Dr. Boudreaux could fit you in," Mom said.

I'd heard Mom's end of the conversation and knew she was more worried than she'd let on. I wasn't upset about my back as much as bummed about my phone call with Coach Buchanan. She'd understood about my injury, but like me, had been disappointed. "Don't sweat it, Kate," she'd said. "Your health is the most important thing. There will be other meets." Sure there would. But at the moment that wasn't much comfort.

The receptionist announced, "Kate Lovejoy, the doctor will see you now."

Mom and I followed a nurse down the hall. She weighed me, took my temperature, and then my blood pressure. "You'll be in the first exam room on the left," she said.

Mom took a seat, while the nurse handed me a paper gown. "Here, it closes in the back."

I quickly changed from my jeans and T-shirt into the flimsy gown. I was so happy Dr. Boudreaux was a woman. My body had just started to change and I was a little self-conscious about it.

I climbed on the examining table, then dangled my feet off the side. Mom picked at her cuticles. "How's your back?" she asked.

"The Tylenol is helping." I didn't want to worry her, so I kept the worst part to myself. When I moved too quickly, it felt like shards of glass were embedded in my muscles.

We heard a knock at the door. "Come in," Mom called.

Dr. Boudreaux had lavender glasses that complemented her green eyes. "How's Chris doing with his allergies?"

"Good. The Flonase is helping," Mom said.

Dr. Boudreaux pulled a chair between Mom and me. "So, tell me what brings you here today."

Mom started with last night and the lump on my shoulder blade.

"It's been going on for a couple of weeks," I admitted.

"A couple of weeks?!" Mom said incredulously. "Why didn't you tell me?"

"I thought it would go away on its own, and then I decided to wait and tell you after my gymnastics meet. I was afraid you wouldn't let me go."

"Well . . . you were *exactly* right about that," Mom said.

Dr. Boudreaux untied the paper gown so she could examine my back and shoulder. "Do you have any other lumps, or is this the only one?"

"I think it's the only one."

She lightly touched my sore spot. "Okay, but I'd like to examine you to be sure. Would that be all right?"

"Yes."

Dr. Boudreaux started by looking at my face, in my ears and mouth. She patted my neck and ran her hands up and down my arms and legs.

When she finished, she gave me a reassuring smile. "The good news is everything else seems normal." She glanced over at Mom. "I'm not sure what's wrong with Kate's shoulder blade, so I'm going to send her to a pediatric orthopedist."

Mom didn't say a word, but the worry lines etched across her forehead made my heart beat faster.

NO MORE SECRETS

I was lying on my right side, wishing the lump on my shoulder would magically disappear, when Chris knocked on my door. "Sorry about your gymnastics meet."

"Thanks."

"Since you can't jump on the trampoline, want to play video games?"

"Maybe later."

I thought about Claire, Nat, and Jayla—how they were competing and cheering each other on. Tears leaked from the corners of my eyes, but I kept my back to Chris so that he couldn't see them.

"Mom's making chicken noodle soup," he said.

Any time Chris or I got sick, Mom made us soup. Pretty soon the house would smell amazing.

"I'm not hungry. I just want to nap."

As Chris pulled the door shut, I closed my eyes and felt the pain pills Dr. Boudreaux had prescribed finally kick in. I had an appointment scheduled on Wednesday with the orthopedist. Four days seemed like forever. I tried telling myself the lump was no big deal, but deep down I knew better. Dr. Boudreaux and Mom had both looked worried.

After my nap, I had some soup and then watched TV with Mom, Dad, and Chris.

Instead of arguing over the remote like he usually did, Chris passed it to me. Jonathan from *Property Brothers* was demo-ing a kitchen. It would make me feel better if I could swing a sledgehammer and help him.

"Okay, that's enough," Mom said, taking the remote from my hand. "You barely touched your soup, and your face is drooping like an old hound dog."

"Don't pick on my girl," Dad said. "She's entitled to mope around a little."

"Being miserable for the next four days will only

make things worse," Mom said. "There's no use worrying until we know exactly what we're dealing with, which is probably nothing."

Mom's hands were trembling, though, which shredded the little confidence I had left.

"Done!" Chris said, waving his cell phone in the air. "I sent Mindy a text and she'll be here in half an hour to bake cookies with Kate."

That was an awesome idea, but I couldn't resist teasing him. "You can't fool me. I know you have a crush on Mindy."

Chris blushed beet red, and Mom and Dad laughed.

"Of course he has a crush on her," Dad said. "Mindy's cute."

While I waited for Mindy, I got out the recipe for Martha Stewart's Best Ever Sugar Cookies. The recipe was a specialty of ours. Mindy and I made sugar cookies at Christmas in the shapes of pine trees, bells, and gingerbread men, we made football jerseys for the Super Bowl, hearts for Valentine's Day, and for Halloween ghosts, bats, and pumpkins.

"Hey," Mindy said, standing in the kitchen doorway. "How are you feeling?" Like me, she was wearing her oldest jeans, an LSU T-shirt, and had her hair pulled back in a ponytail. We could have been twins.

"Sore."

"Sorry about that. Why didn't you tell me? I had no idea until I got a text from Chris."

I tried to shrug, but instead winced when a sharp pain ran down my arm.

"I told *you* about my dad," Mindy reminded me. A couple of years ago, Mindy's dad had called unexpectedly. He'd asked how she was doing in school, and if she remembered him. There was no way she could have—he'd left when she was a baby.

"I didn't mean to hurt your feelings. I just didn't want to talk about it. I want it to go away."

Mindy held out her little finger for a pinkie swear. "No more secrets?"

I wrapped my finger around hers. "No more secrets." The lump on my shoulder hadn't magically disappeared, but at least I had my best friend to make cookies with.

ONE STEP CLOSER

The waiting room was crowded. I sat on a love seat between Mom and Dad, squeezed like the filling in an Oreo. I needed to know what was wrong with me.

Dr. Williams was running late. Zoning out, I thought about the cookies I'd baked with Mindy. We'd made them shaped like pumpkins and leaves, then iced them with orange and yellow frosting. I hadn't been able to whisk together the dry ingredients or spread the dough with the rolling pin. Mindy had done both of those things, and I'd used the cookie cutters, which didn't take much arm strength.

Claire, Nat, and Jayla had all won medals at the gymnastics meet. I was happy our team had done so well, and at the same time, jealous. At school, my teammates had been great, though; Claire had even offered to carry my books.

"Kate Lovejoy," the receptionist called.

"Ready?" Mom asked. She squeezed my clammy hand.

I didn't know which was worse—to dread a bad diagnosis, or to actually have one.

"I'll be out here if you need me," Dad said.

The appointment began like every other appointment in my life—weight, height, blood pressure, and temperature. The only difference was I'd never been this nervous before.

A couple of minutes later, we met Dr. Williams. He had bushy gray eyebrows that reminded me of a caterpillar. "So, tell me about your back," he said.

I repeated everything I'd already told Dr. Boudreaux. That my pain seemed to come and go. How it moved around. That my back had been achy for a couple of weeks, and there had been some swelling.

"A couple of weeks?" His eyebrows arched and I couldn't stop looking at them.

"I was going to tell Mom after my gymnastics meet, but I woke up with a lump instead."

"Mind if I take a look?"

He ran his fingers across my back, gently touching the lump. "I'm going to order X-rays and see if we can tell what's going on in there. Mrs. Lovejoy, does she have any other orthopedic problems I should be aware of?"

Mom shook her head and smiled. "Nothing except her funny toes."

"Funny toes?" Dr. Williams's caterpillar eyebrows drew close together. "While you're here, I might as well take a look at them."

My big toes were short and curved inward. They'd been that way since I was born but hadn't been a problem.

"Looks like bunions," Dr. Williams said. "Let's X-ray her toes too."

He kept staring at them, but I didn't mind. X-rays were much better than being stuck with needles, getting stitches, or having some kind of surgery. X-rays wouldn't hurt at all.

Two days later, Dr. Williams called Mom. He recommended I see yet another doctor—this time a geneticist.

Now I was really scared.

IT'S A ZEBRA

A nurse led Mom, Dad, and me to Dr. Chen's office. She had short, spiky hair that reminded me of a singer in a punk rock band.

Dr. Chen asked a lot of questions about our family medical history. It was long and boring. I just wanted to know what was wrong with me. Finally, she pulled my X-rays from an oversized manila folder, then put them on a lighted screen. "Kate's big toes are malformed, plus she has ossification—new bone growth—on her left shoulder blade. Both those things are indicative of a rare genetic disorder called Fibrodysplasia Ossificans Progressiva."

"I . . . I've never heard of that before," Mom said. "What is it?"

Dad had brought along a notepad and pencil. His breath was fast and furious as he took notes.

I caught snippets:

One of the rarest disorders in the world.

Turns muscle and soft connective tissue into bone.

Affects mobility.

Flare-ups often caused by trauma.

Doctors can't predict when or how much a body will be affected.

Most sports not advisable.

"What?" I asked. "You mean . . . you mean I can't do gymnastics?" It didn't seem real, more like a TV medical drama that was happening to someone else.

Dr. Chen shook her head. "I'm sorry, but I don't think gymnastics is a good idea."

Dad's pencil snapped in two.

I focused on the pencil.

"I don't mean to doubt your expertise," Dad said, "but have you ever seen this condition before?"

"No. FOP is extremely rare; most doctors will never encounter it."

"Maybe we should get a second opinion," Mom said. Her body shook like a mini-earthquake.

Dr. Chen leaned toward us with her hands clasped on her desk. "I would recommend genetic testing to confirm my diagnosis, but I'm confident it's correct. And as for a second opinion, the world's preeminent expert is Dr. Fred Kaplan at the University of Pennsylvania School of Medicine. I have already called him about Kate. He'd be happy to speak with you."

She'd already called him? This must be really bad. Mom and Dad kept asking questions, but I didn't hear most of them. The blizzard inside of me drowned them out. I caught the word *zebra*. "Zebra? What does a zebra have to do with my back?"

"'When you hear hoofs, think horse, not zebra,'" Dr. Chen repeated. "It means patients usually have a common diagnosis, but FOP is a zebra. The odds of it affecting you are one in two million."

Dad looked so pale, it scared me. "One in two *million*?" he asked.

"Yes, and to carry the analogy further, just like no two zebras have identical stripes, no two people with FOP experience it exactly the same way."

Dr. Chen had made a terrible mistake. There was no way I had this awful disease that I'd never even heard of. "I want to go home!"

Dad reached out and squeezed my hand. "In just a

49

minute. We need Dr. Kaplan's contact information."

"I think Kate has had enough," Mom said. "We'll be in the waiting room."

She followed me out, leaving Dad alone with Dr. Chen. I didn't stop at the waiting room; I bolted for the parking lot. I needed to breathe.

CHARLIE

Simone, Aly, and Gabby, smiling and perfect in their leotards—I couldn't stand to look at them anymore. With my good arm, I ripped their posters from my walls, then stomped on them.

"Kate," Mom called. "Unlock your door!"

"No!" I shouted.

"We need to talk," Mom said.

I ignored her and pulled Simone's autobiography from my bookshelf. I knew exactly what I was looking for, a quote near the front by Mary Lou Retton. *When I give motivational talks to young people, I tell them that if they truly believe in themselves, and are willing to put in the effort, they can achieve anything.*

What a joke. What a big fat lie. I ripped the page in two!

"Chris is going to jimmy the lock," Mom warned.

I hurled Simone's book at my full-length mirror. It bounced off and landed with a thud.

"What are you doing in there?" Mom yelled.

As she and Chris barreled in, I kneeled and scooted to the farthest corner of my closet.

"Whoa," Mom said incredulously. "You cracked the mirror."

I didn't care . . . not even a little bit.

Chris got on his hands and knees and crawled in beside me. "Want some company?" he whispered.

"Yeah, but can you get rid of Mom?"

"Hey, Mom, I need to talk to Kate alone. How about making us some popcorn?"

"Popcorn? Kate's having a meltdown and you want me to make popcorn?!"

"Yes," Chris answered. "With lots of butter."

A smile tugged at my lips.

"Okay, fine. I'll make the darned popcorn, but after it pops, Kate has to come out of the closet. She's worrying me."

As soon as Mom left, Chris put his arm around my shoulders. "Your talent was wasted on gymnastics. You should have been a baseball pitcher."

I snorted. "I shouldn't have been anything. I shouldn't have even been born."

"Ah, Kate, don't say that."

"Well, it's how I feel."

"If there were no Kate, I'd be lonely," he said.

A tear trickled down my cheek.

"I've got an idea," Chris said. "I know Chloe mostly belonged to you, but you're not the only one who misses her. Let's adopt a rescue dog."

"No."

"Ah, c'mon, Kate. There's a dog out there that needs rescuing. I'll even let you pick it."

My heart melted as I thought about snuggling with Chloe, of her following me everywhere I went, of her sleeping at the foot of my bed.

"You know it's a good idea," Chris said.

I sighed. "Maybe, but don't get your hopes up." It was just like Chris not to mention FOP. I bet he didn't know what to say about it any more than I did, but underneath the anger, I was really scared.

Going to the animal shelter was a family event. Mom, Dad, and Chris were excited. I worried about not finding a dog I would love as much as Chloe.

A chubby woman with short purple hair sat behind a metal desk. "Can I help you?"

"We called earlier about adopting a dog," Dad said.

While he chatted with the receptionist, my mind wandered. It had been a strange week at school. My parents had agreed not to tell anyone about my FOP until we understood more about it. Dad had talked with Dr. Fred at the University of Pennsylvania School of Medicine, and Mom was reading the *FOP Handbook*. I was still trying to pretend FOP didn't exist, but I had lost some reach in my left arm. I couldn't raise it over my head or put it behind my back, which meant no PE or gymnastics practice. Coach B. still thought it was because of an injury.

We followed the purple-haired woman to the kennel area. Some dogs barked, others whimpered. Most raised on their hind legs to peer at us through their crates, but one dog didn't move or make a peep. "What's wrong with him?" I asked.

"Charlie's sad," the purple-haired woman said. "His owner died from cancer, and her family brought him here."

Charlie was pretty small—not even knee-high and probably about ten pounds. He had a beautiful coat:

tan with some white, black, and dark brown. "What kind of dog is he?"

"A Lhasa Apso mix."

Mom, Dad, and Chris stayed quiet while the lady opened Charlie's crate. "Would you like to hold him?"

I froze, afraid my arm wouldn't support his weight.

"Here, let me," Chris said. He stepped forward and cuddled Charlie to his chest.

Though Chris was holding Charlie, the little dog kept looking at me. I scratched behind his ears, then rubbed his back.

"Lhasa Apsos are originally from Tibet," the woman said. "They were known for being watchdogs in palaces and monasteries. They're highly protective of their owners."

"Any downsides to the breed?" Dad asked.

"They have a lot of hair and require daily brushing and combing."

I shook my head. My arm hurt too much for all that brushing and combing. "We need a dog with short hair," I said.

Charlie whimpered.

"We can all help with the brushing and combing," Mom said.

"No, I need a dog I can take care of myself."

I bent down to tell Charlie goodbye and he licked my face.

Doggy kisses.

Chloe used to kiss me exactly the same way. My heart grew in my chest like the Grinch who stole Christmas, and I couldn't resist Charlie for another second.

He was my dog now.

A FAMILY MEETING

That evening, a storm blew in off the gulf—the kind of night to get comfy and cozy. Mom made hot chocolate while I searched for a bag of marshmallows. "Hey, Mom, if the rain lets up, can I invite Mindy over to meet Charlie?"

"Not tonight. Dad and I are calling a family meeting."

Our last family meeting had been about moving from West Virginia to Baton Rouge. I could still picture our old house and remember the sad, anxious feelings about leaving Grandma and Grandpa. "Are we moving again?"

"No. It's to discuss FOP. Dad and I have scheduled a follow-up appointment with your geneticist."

"I don't want to go."

Mom nodded. "That's fine. But during the first meeting Dad and I didn't ask enough questions. We need to fully understand FOP so we can make the best decisions for you and our family."

Having FOP meant I was different than every other kid I knew. I had stood in this same spot and pinkie-swore not to keep secrets from Mindy, but I had broken my promise. Telling anybody, even her, would make it real.

Mom put our mugs on a tray and carried them into the family room. Dad immediately switched off the TV.

I wished he hadn't. Our house was never this quiet.

Mom and Dad sat side by side on the sofa. Chris and I rocked in matching swivel chairs; Charlie lay at my feet. "Dad and I have been researching FOP and talking to experts," Mom said. "Do either of you have any questions about it?"

"I do," Chris said. "Is it possible I have it too?"

Dad shook his head. "Your toes are normal. Besides, neither your mom nor I have FOP. Most cases are like Kate's—a genetic mutation."

Great—I was a mutant. Dad's words echoed in my

mind. *Neither your mom nor I have FOP.* "Wait!" I said. "If I have kids, will they have FOP?"

"They would have a fifty-fifty chance," Mom said.

A steady rain beat against the windowpanes. Lightning streaked across the sky. The storm outside was mild compared to the one that raged inside of me.

"The main thing you kids need to be aware of," Dad said, "is that trauma can make FOP worse. So, no roughhousing. As much as possible, Kate needs to avoid bumps and falls."

"Shots can cause flare-ups too," Mom said. "Any doctor or dentist who treats Kate from now on will need to be educated about FOP."

"What about the trampoline, or sports?" I asked.

Dad placed his hot chocolate on the coffee table and leaned forward. "No two families handle risk the same way. Your mom and I read about a young man with FOP who went bungee jumping. His parents allowed him to do as much as he could as long as he was able. We've read about other parents who've banned bikes, scooters, and monkey bars. There is no right answer, and Kate, most times it will be up to you. Your mom and I won't be at school with you, or at Girl Scout meetings, or sleepovers."

I didn't have enough reach to swing a bat or a tennis racket. I couldn't do a push-up or a jumping jack. I needed to avoid being hit with a dodge ball. Other than walking around the track or the gym, I didn't see how I could participate in PE. "How are the doctors going to fix my arm?"

Mom's eyes got teary. "Bean, I'm so sorry, but they can't fix it."

"What about surgery?" I asked.

"Surgery is not an option," Dad said. "The trauma would most likely cause a flare-up and your body would make even more bone where it's not supposed to."

"So . . . my arm is just going to be like this?" This crazy thing couldn't be happening to me.

"For now," Dad said, "but there's always hope. The research team at UPenn is hard at work to find a cure for FOP."

But . . .

Research takes a lot of money . . . and a long time.

My arm was partially frozen, and it could get worse.

I didn't realize I'd whimpered until Charlie whimpered too.

AN IEP

took Charlie for a long walk to put off reading the *FOP Handbook*. I had insisted Mom let me read it. I needed to read it, but once I knew the stuff inside, I wouldn't be able to pretend anymore.

Down by the lake, Charlie barked at a squirrel and snuffled through acorns and dried oak leaves. Chris had been exactly right about rescuing a dog. Now that I didn't have gymnastics practice, walking Charlie gave me something else to do.

Mom was getting her notes together for a school meeting. She wanted to educate all my teachers, the school nurse, and the administrators about FOP so I could be part of the Individualized Education Program. I didn't think it was necessary, at least not yet, but Mom hadn't listened.

The meeting was scheduled for next week. I needed to tell Mindy and the rest of my friends before then, but how? I didn't know what to say—I was worried about being different.

"You're not giving your friends enough credit," Mom had said, but I knew classmates with disabilities were often ignored. Rather than trying to talk to them and saying the wrong thing, it was easier to say nothing at all.

I sat down on a wooden bench by the lake, then scratched Charlie behind his ears. "I love you, Charlie."

"Arf arf!" The best thing about dogs is unconditional love. No matter what happened with my FOP, Charlie would treat me the same way. He'd get excited every time I walked through the door. Humans could learn a lot from dogs.

Mom had moved on from the *FOP Handbook* to a memoir called *Finding Magic Mountain*. The author was a mom too, and her son Vincent had FOP. "This book gives me hope," Mom had said. "Vincent graduated from medical school. That shows that despite FOP, you can still have a very bright future."

Vincent's *bright future* made Mom feel better, but I was still mad.

"Nobody's future is certain," Mom had said.

She was right, but without breakthrough research, my FOP would get worse. What if I ended up in a wheelchair, or unable to comb my hair, or needed help going to the bathroom? I wanted my old life back. I wanted to be a gymnastics champion. I didn't want to imagine a future with FOP.

After our walk, Charlie trailed me to my room like a shadow. Mom had placed the *FOP Handbook* on my nightstand. I had already read a booklet called *What Is FOP? Questions and Answers for the Children*, but it wasn't enough. When I'd asked Mom if I could read the same book she was reading, she'd hesitated. "How about we read it together?" she'd finally said.

"No," I'd argued. "This isn't like *Harry Potter*." Mom and I had taken turns reading *Harry* out loud to each other. Then, softly, I asked, "Mom, is there something in the handbook you don't want me to know about?"

"Ah, Bean, I'm sorry for giving you that impression. It's the same material, just presented in more depth, and in more grown-up language."

"Then why can't I read it?"

"You win," Mom said. "I'll leave it on your night-stand."

Charlie looked up at me, then barked. I couldn't think of a single human being I wanted to share the handbook with, but I didn't have to read it alone.

I propped both pillows behind my back and snuggled with Charlie on my bed. The first sentence was, *Life doesn't prepare you for Fibrodysplasia Ossificans Progressiva.* That was the truest sentence I'd ever read.

There was a note to readers about processing the information in the book gradually. No way. It had been hard enough to find the courage to get started.

The book said I'd been lucky to get a correct diagnosis. Some kids had been misdiagnosed. They'd had needless surgeries and even chemotherapies.

Charlie put his head in my lap, a signal for me to scratch behind his ears. As long as I needed him, he would stay right beside me.

I read that a person with FOP can go months, or even years, without a flare-up. I stopped and prayed. "Please help me not have any more flare-ups."

Chapter two was called "Things to Avoid and Alternatives." Mom and Dad had already gone over most of that information: avoid bumps, falls, intramuscular injections, and elective surgery.

One sentence felt like somebody had squeezed my heart. *A flare-up can strike mysteriously for no reason at all.* I could be as careful as careful could be. I could do everything right and still have a flare-up. It wasn't fair.

"Kate?" Mom hurried across the room and hugged me. "Kate, can I come in?"

"Just a sec." I reached for a Kleenex to wipe my eyes.

"I'm making Grandma's mac and cheese for dinner. I thought you deserved a treat."

"Thanks. Have you told Grandma and Grandpa about my FOP?"

"Not yet, but soon. How far have you gotten in the handbook?"

"I'm reading about flare-ups. How they can last six weeks or more. That's a long time."

"It *is* a long time," Mom agreed.

"But that's not even the worst part. There is no medicine to stop my body from making more bone."

"Ah, Bean. The glass is still half-full. Think of it this way: At least there's medicine to minimize the flare-ups and relieve some of the pain."

"It still stinks."

Mom reached out to hug me again . . . that's when I started to cry.

THE ASSIGNMENT

While Mrs. Landry and the rest of my classmates discussed *Evangeline of the Bayou*, I stared out the window. How was I supposed to care about Evangeline's problems when I had bigger ones of my own?

Mom said our trampoline had to go. After she read that swimming was a good activity for kids with FOP, she and Dad decided to get rid of the trampoline and put in a pool. Mindy had been in awe when I told her.

"Wow," she'd said. "I didn't know your family was *that* rich."

If Mindy had been the one diagnosed with FOP, she wouldn't be getting a pool.

Mrs. Landry pushed her long, wavy hair over her shoulders. I bet she'd never considered how lucky she was that both her arms worked.

"Class, your next essay will be titled 'If I Could Change the World.' You'll have two weeks to decide on a topic. Choose one thing you'd change, and then explain why it's important to you."

"How long does the essay have to be?" Izaak asked.

"A two-hundred-and-fifty-word minimum. All topics have to be approved by me beforehand."

"I'm going to write about my quest to become a world class gymnast," Claire said.

"Hmmm," Mrs. Landry said. "That would change *your* life, but how would it change the world?"

"What about ending world hunger?" Jayla asked.

"That's a good topic," Mrs. Landry agreed, "but you need to dig deeper. Tell me why it's important to you. Have you ever worked at a soup kitchen, or had a personal connection to a family without enough to eat?"

Jayla shook her head.

I wanted to write about finding a cure for FOP, but that wouldn't really change the world. Only the world for me and 3,500 other unlucky people. Dad had said finding a cure might also benefit people who have weak bones, like women with osteoporosis. I wondered if adding people with weak bones would make the topic work for Mrs. Landry.

I kept thinking and made a connection. If I could find the right subject, I could write a paper for English class, and then also use it to make my speech for Girl Scouts. *Write about something you believe in.* I needed a topic I believed in that had the potential to change the world. I knew exactly who could help me find it.

My pediatrician had written a note excusing me from PE, so I had a free study period in the library. "Hi, Kate," our librarian said. "How's your arm?"

Ms. Batiste always dressed in beautiful colors. Today she had on a gold blouse. "It's about the same," I told her.

"Oh ... I'm sorry to hear that. Are you going to physical therapy?"

"No," and then I blurted out, "I have this weird disease, and physical therapy can make it worse."

"Do you want to talk about it?"

"I guess." I sat down at one of the tables, then Ms. Batiste took the seat across from me.

"Does this disease have a name?"

I couldn't look her in the eye. Instead, I focused on the beads that hung on the ends of her box braids. "Fibrodysplasia Ossificans Progressiva."

"Wow. That's a mouthful."

I told Ms. Batiste everything. About the lump, and seeing three different doctors, and all the things I'd read in the handbook. "Nobody at school knows yet, but Mom has a meeting scheduled next week to tell all my teachers."

"I'm going to research FOP," Ms. Batiste said. "That way I can be a more effective ally for you. Is there anything else I can do to help?"

"Yes. Could you brainstorm with me? I have to write a paper about changing the world."

"I can't tell you what to write about," Ms. Batiste said, "but it should be something that comes from the heart. If I had to write such a paper, I'd choose how to make the world a more equitable place for people like me—Black people."

"Yeah, Izaak's dad is afraid for him to be out at night in our white neighborhood."

Ms. Batiste nodded. "That's exactly what I'm talking about. Izaak could write about that topic in a more authentic way than a white person. What could you write authentically about, Kate?"

"I'm not sure. That's the problem. Maybe something to do with FOP."

"Sounds like you're on the right track," Ms. Batiste said. "Why don't you sleep on it?"

MINDY'S BIRTHDAY

It was Mindy's birthday, and Mateo Diaz and I had been invited over for dinner. I didn't know whether to tell Mindy about FOP or put it off for a while longer. I had promised no secrets, but Mindy's birthday should be a celebration, and FOP was a downer.

"Don't forget to walk Charlie first," Mom reminded me.

I whistled, then fastened the leash to his collar. I bent down, showing Charlie my new bracelet. "It's a MedicAlert." The front had a snake wrapped around a staff, and the back said, *Excessive bone formation due to genetic disorder. Must handle gently.*

Charlie looked at me with his intelligent brown eyes and answered with a woof.

We took a left turn down by the lake. "I'm having trouble paying attention in class," I told him.

Charlie stopped, then nuzzled my leg. He knew I needed a hug.

"That's not my biggest problem, though. The biggest problem is I'm a chicken. I haven't told Mindy or any of my other friends about FOP."

Charlie's ears perked up, so I could tell he was listening.

"I've been reading about this boy, Ollie Collins. FOP doesn't affect your brain, so he focused on music, drama, and debating rather than sports."

Charlie barked in reply.

"I want to be more like Ollie. He decided what accommodations he needed at school. His parents didn't just take over. I don't want to hurt Mom's feelings, but she needs to ask my opinion. What do you think?"

Charlie wagged his tail, so I knew he agreed with me.

After our walk, I put Charlie in his crate and climbed into Mom's car. I wanted to tell her all of the things I had said to Charlie, but talking to a dog was much easier. The words I wanted to say were bottled up inside. I stayed quiet until Mom parked the car. "Can you carry Mindy's present inside?" I asked her. "I'm afraid of dropping it."

"Sure. It'll give me a chance to wish her a happy birthday."

While Mom chatted with Mrs. Hebert, I said hello to Mateo, who played the flute beside Mindy in band. "Mrs. Hebert made spaghetti and meatballs," he said.

Besides playing the flute, Mateo loved to eat. He could eat an entire pizza all by himself and still have room for dessert.

Mindy threw her arms around my shoulders and gave me a hug. Pain radiated down my arm. It took all my concentration to keep from screaming.

But the whole house smelled wonderful, like basil and tomato sauce. At dinner while I twirled spaghetti around my fork, I watched Mateo and Mindy. He had a crush on her, and *she* had a crush on Chris. It would surely be easier if all crushes were reciprocal.

"I'm practicing my flute every day," Mateo said. "You'd better work hard if you want to keep first chair."

Mindy smiled at him, but it was different than when she smiled at Chris, not as nervous or shy.

"The meatballs are delicious," I said to Mrs. Hebert.

"Glad you like them. Be sure to save room for cake and ice cream."

I couldn't wait for Mindy to open her presents. I'd texted Mateo about my gift, and he'd chosen a present she could use along with mine.

"Kate, have the doctors given you any idea when you can get back to gymnastics?" Mrs. Hebert asked.

Mateo and Mindy both stopped chewing and stared at me.

"Uh . . . umm . . . they're not sure yet, but it'll probably be pretty soon." I slumped in my chair. I should have told the truth, but I didn't want to ruin Mindy's party.

Mateo finished his second serving of spaghetti, and then Mrs. Hebert brought out the cake. It had purple icing, a figure of an astronaut, and letters spelling out *HAPPY BIRTHDAY MINDY!*

I had been waiting to give her my gift for weeks. I hoped she would unwrap it first.

Instead, she opened the gift from her mom. The box was made of royal-blue velvet—the kind you get in a jewelry store. Mindy popped it open and lifted out a necklace—a heart-shaped locket. Inside was a picture of the two of us from space camp.

"Oh, Mom, I really love it!" She passed the locket to Mateo, who took a look and passed it to me. My eyes were on Mindy. I sent her a telegraphic message: Open mine next.

But no, Mindy picked up Mateo's package. She flipped it over, carefully running her fingers along the seam to break the tape. It was a book: *National Geographic's Space Atlas*. "There's a foreword by Buzz Aldrin!" Mindy said.

While she took forever studying the photographs, my heart pounded. I really hoped she would love my present. I really hoped she wouldn't mind that I had bought it used.

Mindy closed the book. "I saved the biggest gift for last."

It had taken me a long time to find the perfect wrapping paper. It was beautiful, black like the night sky and dotted with stars and planets. Mindy ran her fingers along the seam. Finally, I couldn't stand it anymore. "Just rip into it!"

"This paper is too awesome to ruin," Mindy said.

I held my breath as she opened the box.

"Aaah!" Mindy's eyes were shining. "I've always wanted a telescope!"

"That must have been so expensive," Mrs. Hebert said.

"No, I bought it at a yard sale. But Dad checked it out and said it's in perfect shape."

"I can't wait to use it," Mindy said. "Mom, is it okay if we take my book and the telescope outside now?"

"Yes, enjoy yourselves! It won't take me long to clean the kitchen."

Mateo helped Mindy set up the telescope. I hung back, looking at the night sky through my own two eyes. I remembered a nursery rhyme:

Star light, star bright
First star I see tonight,
I wish I may, I wish I might
Have the wish I wish tonight.

LIKE A FREAK

On the drive home from Mindy's party, I decided to free the words bottled inside my chest. "Mom, do you remember reading about Ollie Collins in the *FOP Handbook*?"

"Yes."

"Well . . . I want you to treat me like his mom treats him. You and Dad decided to get rid of the trampoline and put in a pool without talking to me first."

"But you love to swim, and you could get hurt on the trampoline."

"I know, but that's not the point. I want to be included in decisions that affect me."

Mom's hands tightened on the steering wheel, and

she kept her eyes on the road. "Okay," she finally said. "I understand."

"I also read the chapter in the handbook about school. You charged ahead about an IEP without really listening to me. I don't need any accommodations in my academic classes, but I *could* use a rolling backpack so I don't put any more pressure on my shoulder."

"Anything else?"

"Yeah, I want to get my PE credits by swimming."

"I'll talk to your teacher, but make sure you tell me if things change and you need more help."

"It's not *if* things change, but *when*. Don't treat me like a baby, Mom. I'm old enough to understand what *progressive* means."

Mom sucked in her breath as if I'd punched her in the stomach. "I know it's progressive, but I'm hoping it will be years before you have another flare-up." She sighed. "And I'm praying that Dr. Kaplan and his team find a cure."

"Me too. I've been praying to St. Sebastian every day."

"Are you ready for me to call Coach Buchanan?" Mom asked.

Giving up gymnastics was worse than putting my

heart through a paper shredder. I leaned my forehead against the car window, staring out into the darkness. "How about I send Coach B. a text?" I said. "I'll tell her my shoulder is not healing the way we'd like, and so I'm taking a break."

Mom nodded. "Okay, if that makes it easier for you, but the truth is bound to come out."

The truth was like Pandora's box, which we'd learned about in school—telling everyone could bring unexpected problems. "I know, but I want Claire, Nat, and Jayla to hear about FOP from me rather than from Coach Buchanan."

"Have you told Mindy?"

Tears pricked my eyes. "No . . . I thought about doing it tonight, but Mateo was there, and I didn't want to ruin Mindy's birthday."

"You were just being thoughtful," Mom said.

I knew that wasn't the whole story, though. I had always thought of Mindy as my twin, like we were two peas in a pod. I didn't want to be different than her.

The cafeteria was so noisy the next day, it gave me a headache. I pinched the crust off my pimento cheese sandwich while Claire, Nat, and Jayla talked about gymnastics.

"I've been studying Simone Biles on YouTube," Claire said. "Her triple double on floor is amazing. I've watched it about a hundred times."

"That's because she's the GOAT," Nat said.

The GOAT—greatest of all time, a champion, something I'd never get the chance to be. Maybe someday I'd be able to talk about gymnastics without feeling sick to my stomach, but definitely not yet.

"Hey, Kate, do you have a new bracelet?" Jayla asked.

I stared down at my wrist. "It's a MedicAlert bracelet."

"Oh," Jayla said. "Are you allergic to penicillin? That's why my mom wears one."

"No. It's because of my shoulder."

"That's weird," Nat said. "When my brother broke his leg, he didn't have to wear a bracelet."

"This is different."

Nat squinted and her forehead scrunched into wavy lines. "How?"

"I have . . ." I didn't know what to say. "I have . . ." I would have told a lie, but I couldn't think of one fast enough. "I have this . . . rare disease."

Jayla's eyes widened. "Will you be okay?"

"I hope so."

Claire stared at me as if she could see right through my skin to my quivering heart. "What about our gymnastics team?"

"I . . . I have to quit."

"That's terrible," Claire said. "I'd rather die than quit gymnastics!" She clapped her hand over her mouth. "Sorry. I didn't mean to say that."

Nat reached for a napkin and wiped a grape mustache off her upper lip. "What's the disease called?"

"Fibrodysplasia Ossificans Progressiva."

"Fibro Ossifica What?" Nat asked.

"Just call it FOP. Everybody else does, and if you're interested you can read more about it on the internet."

My friends were silent, like when I'd told them Chloe had died. My head ached even worse. "Hey, can y'all quit staring at me?"

Finally, Jayla nodded. "Yeah, ummm, okay, sure. I've already started work on my Book Artist badge. I checked a huge stack of picture books out of the library. The illustrators are really amazing."

Jayla talked nonstop, but it was super awkward. I was sure the girls were all thinking about my rare disorder.

I felt like a freak.

WITH A THUD

When Charlie and I got back from our usual walk, Mom was in the kitchen making dinner. I smelled ground beef and onions cooking. "How was school?" she asked.

Lunch had been awful, but I didn't tell Mom how I'd felt like a freak. She'd worry, and besides, she couldn't fix it. I was ashamed. I wished I could hide FOP in the back of my sock drawer and forget about it. "It was okay."

Mom studied my face while she poured enchilada sauce over the beef. "You don't sound okay. What's wrong, Bean?"

I plopped down in a chair and rested my elbows on

the table. "I told Claire, Jayla, and Nat about FOP, and then everything got all weird."

"It'll get better. I'll bet they didn't know how to respond and were afraid of saying the wrong thing."

"Yeah, probably. At Girl Scouts, I'll show them FOP doesn't have to be such a big deal."

"It might be a big deal for a while," Mom said. "Be patient. These things take time."

After dinner, Mom drove me to Claire's. I didn't say much in the car. I was nervous and determined to act like the old Kate, the one who didn't have FOP.

Claire lived in a large white house that had columns in the front, black shutters, and a deep porch. I used the brass door knocker, reminding myself to smile pretty, act pleasant, and be a good friend. Things I never used to worry about before I told my teammates about FOP. Mom had told me to be patient, but for how long? I was already sick of feeling like a freak.

Mrs. Chevalier answered the door. "Kate! We weren't expecting you. Claire told me about your illness. We thought you'd probably need to rest."

The smile slid from my face. I didn't respond as I followed her to the basement. Claire's younger brother was playing by the steps. Mrs. Chevalier bent down. "Tyler, remember our talk about the Girl Scouts' meeting? Please move your trucks and play quietly over in the corner."

The other Girl Scouts were sitting around card tables and Nat waved me over. Claire sort of half winced/half smiled at me, as if I had cooties. Jayla had brought along a couple of picture books. She looked up from flipping through one. "Hi, Kate, we saved you a seat, just in case you were feeling up to coming."

Mrs. Chevalier and my friends were acting like I was ready for the graveyard, but I decided to ignore it. "What are you reading?"

"*She Persisted: Thirteen American Women Who Changed the World*. It's by Chelsea Clinton."

"Are you trying to cut the work in half by combining your Girl Scouts' badge with your English assignment?"

Jayla nodded. "I'm passionate about art and it can change the world. How'd you guess?"

"Because I have a similar idea."

Since Claire and Nat were journaling, I picked up the other book Jayla had brought along: *All the Way to the Top: How One Girl's Fight for Americans with Disabilities Changed Everything.*

I looked up from reading. Claire, Nat, and Jayla were all staring at me.

"I . . . I didn't bring that book on purpose," Jayla said. "I mean, I didn't bring it because of FOP. I'm just reading picture books about changing the world, and I didn't think. I'm really sorry."

My face felt hot. "That never even occurred to me. I picked it up because the rest of you were busy."

"Well, she's sorry," Claire said. "We're all sorry. We read about FOP online, and . . . and . . . it's awful. I saw a picture of a man who's permanently bent over." She stood up and folded her body so that her waist and hips formed a ninety-degree angle. "Like this."

My face felt even hotter, like somebody had set it on fire.

"One more thing," Claire said. "I really messed up. Mom and I ran into Mindy at the pharmacy. I didn't realize you hadn't told her."

"You told *Mindy*?"

"Yeah, but I didn't know," Claire repeated. "She got really angry and called me a liar."

I wanted to slap Claire right across her hateful face. "I . . . I . . . I . . . need to go home. I'll see you girls at school tomorrow."

I hurried toward the steps. I had promised not to keep secrets from Mindy. I had to call her right away and explain what happened.

"Watch out!" Claire yelled.

"Be careful!" Mrs. Chevalier screamed.

It was too late. I stumbled over a toy truck and landed with a thud.

TRAUMA

I lay facedown on the carpet, afraid to move. *No bumps, no falls, no trauma.* Those words were tattooed on my brain, but I'd fallen anyway. My knees and elbows throbbed.

"Kate, are you all right?" Mrs. Chevalier asked.

Claire, Nat, and Jayla formed a half circle around me. Jayla reached out her hand to help me get up.

The girls at the other card tables were watching. Their whispers sounded like bees swarming a nest.

"I'm calling your mother right away," Mrs. Chevalier said.

Nat had tears in her eyes. "How can we help?"

More than anything, I wanted to avoid a flare-up. I was thankful I'd read the *FOP Handbook* and knew about RICE.

Rest: *Minimize movement of injured body part.*

Ice: *Apply a cold pack.*

Compression: *Apply light pressure to the affected body part.*

Elevate: *Raise the body part to help decrease swelling.*

"Could . . . could you get me an ice pack?" I hated the way my voice sounded, scared and shaky.

"Maybe not an ice pack, but I'll find something," Claire said.

I climbed the stairs, clutching at the railing. *No bumps, no falls, no trauma.* I had no way of knowing what FOP would do next. It could freeze my arms straight as sticks, or permanently bent. It could freeze my knees so that I walked with a limp, or not at all. My insides quivered like Jell-O.

I waited for Mom to arrive, lying on the couch in Claire's family room. Nat had wrapped two bags of frozen peas in dishtowels and was holding them against my knees.

Jayla stood by the window watching for Mom.

"Where's Claire?" I asked.

"Mrs. Chevalier asked her to run the Girl Scouts'

meeting and keep an eye on her brother," Nat said.

I stared at Mrs. Chevalier. She was in the next room on her phone, pacing.

"Who is she talking to?" I whispered.

"Claire's dad," Nat whispered back. "She's telling him about your accident."

I overheard the word *liability*, and then Mrs. Chevalier closed the door.

As a precaution, Mom insisted I stay home from school, elevate my legs, and ice my knees and elbows the next day. Charlie didn't care why I was home. He was just happy to cuddle beside me.

Mom stuck her head in my bedroom door. She hadn't slept much. I could tell by the dark circles under her eyes. "How are you feeling?"

"Pretty good, but still nervous I'll have a flare-up."

"Try to relax," Mom said. "A three-day dose of prednisone will hopefully keep that from happening."

The problem was, like most drugs, prednisone had side effects. Dad said the most common were weight gain and mood changes, but they were temporary, while growing new bone definitely wasn't.

Mom walked over and sat on the edge of my bed. "I called Mrs. Hebert. I told her about your fall, and that you hadn't wanted to spoil Mindy's birthday by talking about FOP."

"Mindy's mad at me. I tried calling her last night, but she didn't answer."

"Mrs. Hebert took her phone away for yelling at Claire."

"Yeah, well, Claire deserved it."

Mom winced. "Maybe not this time. It's human nature to talk about bad news, and Claire had every reason to think you would have already told Mindy."

I rolled over so that my back was to Mom. I hadn't told her how Claire had imitated the man with FOP. "I guess you're right."

Mom reached out and ruffled my hair. "Don't waste your energy worrying about what happened yesterday. Instead, think about what you want to say to Mindy. Mrs. Hebert agreed she can have dinner with us tonight."

Mindy still had on her clothes from school—a navy polo shirt and khaki shorts. "Mind if I close the door?" she said.

I'd showered and put on gym shorts and a T-shirt, but I was still propped up in bed. "No, I don't mind."

Mindy closed the door, then leaned against it. "I

hated hearing about your FOP from Claire." Her voice was soft and sad. If she cried, then I'd feel like a total jerk.

"At first I didn't believe Claire, because you'd promised not to keep secrets. But FOP seemed too weird to be a made-up story."

"I was going to tell you," I said, "but I didn't want to ruin your birthday." Mindy had looked so happy—totally different than the sad face she had on now. "I bought the telescope weeks ago. I could hardly wait for you to open it. I didn't plan to tell anyone before you, but Jayla noticed my MedicAlert bracelet. I'm really sorry."

"It's okay," Mindy said. "I got mad because it's easier than being scared—at least that's what Mom thinks. Sort of like how staying mad at Dad is easier than letting him hurt me."

"I'm scared too."

"Anybody would be," Mindy said. "I want to fix it even more than I want a dad who lives with us."

"Ah, Min. You can't fix it. Not even my mom can." I remembered the drive home last night. Mom had cried.

She'd said, "I hate FOP. I wish I had it instead of you."

"Tell me what to do," Mindy pleaded.

I stared into her hazel eyes that looked blue because of her navy shirt. "Just keep being my friend. Claire, Nat, and Jayla don't know what to say to me anymore. They act like I'm dying."

"That's terrible," Mindy said. She walked over to my bed and held out her pinkie. "I promise to treat you the same as always, if you promise to tell me when I mess up."

I wrapped my pinkie around hers. "And I promise the same thing—to treat you like always, if you'll tell me when *I* mess up."

That felt like a true promise—the best kind.

MRS. CHEVALIER

Mom's shrill voice penetrated the wall between our bedrooms. "You're worried about the *liability*? Are you kidding me? Don't you think Kate has enough problems without you adding to them?"

Concentrating on Mom's side of the conversation, I sat up and propped the pillows behind my back.

"No, I will not calm down! How would you feel if it were Claire?"

Ahhh, Mom was talking to Mrs. Chevalier.

The last time I'd heard Mom this angry, a teacher had accused Chris of cheating. The teacher hadn't believed he had written his short story assignment on his own, but she had been wrong. Chris had a great imagination.

"Sure, Kate could join another Girl Scout troop, but her friends are in *your* troop."

Another troop?

"You're being ridiculous," Mom said. "We're not going to sue you. Kate has really been looking forward to the swamp tour."

I climbed out of bed and hurried to Mom's room. When she turned to look at me, I furiously shook my head. Even if Mrs. Chevalier changed her mind, the field trip had been ruined for me. I remembered reading on the website that the swamp had over two hundred species of birds. There were wild pigs and alligators too, but not even an alligator was as mean as Mrs. Chevalier.

"I have to go now," Mom said, but I didn't wait for her to say goodbye. I rushed back to my room and pulled the covers over my head. Gymnastics and Girl Scouts were the two biggest things I had in common with Claire, Nat, and Jayla. What would we talk about at lunch?

And that's when having FOP really sank in. The lunch conversations wouldn't change. They'd just go on without me.

Mom pulled the covers down and tucked them around my shoulders. "Talk to me, Kate."

Her eyes were red from crying. FOP affected me the most, but it also wounded everyone who loved me, especially Mom and Dad. I didn't know what to say. Expressing all my hurt and anger would just make Mom feel worse. "Please don't argue with Mrs. Chevalier anymore."

"That witch made me so mad. It's not very mature of me, but I'd like to kick her in the shins."

A little smile snuck across my face at the thought of Mom acting like an angry kid. "Even if you won the fight, Girl Scouts wouldn't be the same."

"It's not a problem with Girl Scouts," Mom said. "It's a problem with Mrs. Chevalier. I know you were looking forward to the swamp tour, and Dad and I can still take you. You could even invite Mindy."

"Stop trying to make me feel better. It won't work."

Mom walked over to my window and looked out. "The backyard is a mess, but the pool is coming along nicely. Are you still upset we didn't check with you about it?"

I shook my head. "No, a pool isn't the same as a trampoline, but I'm still looking forward to swimming in it."

"Good girl. FOP is going to require a lot of that: focusing on what you can do, rather than what you can't. Want some lunch?"

"Can I have a hot dog and a milkshake?"

"I'll make anything you want," Mom said. "After dealing with Mrs. Chevalier, I could use a treat myself. I'll put double chocolate in the milkshakes."

After Mom left to make lunch, I opened the FOP website: ifopa.org. I clicked on *Just Diagnosed*. In bold letters it said: Remember that you are not alone.

MY FRIEND AMIE

Remember that you are not alone. I kept staring at those words. Of course I wasn't alone. I had Mom and Dad and Chris and Mindy, but still, they didn't have FOP. In fact, I didn't know anyone else who did. I kept reading, searching for anything that might help me, and then, there it was—a mentorship program. Maybe that was the answer! But when I studied the contact information, I discovered I wasn't eligible because both the mentor and the mentee had to be at least eighteen years old. I was only twelve. I mumbled a few words that would have gotten me grounded if either of my parents had heard them.

There had to be something out there. I kept digging

until I found a Facebook group for women living with FOP. I wasn't a woman quite yet, but close enough. I clicked *join*.

But the administrator told me that members have to be at least thirteen.

I closed my laptop with a huff, then cuddled with Charlie. He didn't care about stupid rules.

A few minutes later, I contacted the administrator again. "I just found out I have FOP. I'm really mature for my age and could use a friend."

"*You'll need parental permission,*" she responded.

Soon Mom checked in with the administrator while I wrote an introduction. Although it was short, I spent a long time on it because I didn't want to sound like a little kid.

> *Hi, my name is Kate Lovejoy. I am twelve years old and recently diagnosed with FOP. I live in Baton Rouge, Louisiana, with my mom, dad, brother, Chris, and our dog, Charlie. I'm looking for a friend to private message with. Somebody who has had FOP for a while and wouldn't mind answering a lot of questions.*

An hour later, a woman named Amie Specht responded.

Hi Kate,

We seem to have a lot in common. I'm thirty-five years old and was diagnosed with FOP when I was four. I live in North Carolina now, but like you, I grew up in Louisiana. I love dogs and have two of them—Lilybet and Charlyze. I'm happy to answer any questions that you have about living with FOP.

Your friend,

Amie

Amie. The spelling was unusual, so I looked it up. The name Amie means *friend* in French! It seemed like a sign, as if I had asked for a friend and then God—or St. Sebastian or the universe—had sent one to me. I had so many questions for Amie, I didn't know where to start. Questions like:

How were you diagnosed?

Did kids at school treat you differently because of FOP?

Did FOP keep you from having a boyfriend? (I'm afraid I'll never have one.)

What did you do about PE classes?

How bad is your FOP? (I'm worried about mine getting worse.)

Does prednisone make you feel all moody and sad?

Did you go to college?

Do you have a job?

Did you ever get married?

How do you stop from being afraid all the time?

I wanted to know all of that and more, but I didn't want Amie to think I was nosy, so instead I wrote back:

Dear Amie,

Thank you for being my friend. I have A LOT of questions but thought maybe we should get to know each other first. My favorite TV show is Say Yes to the Dress. *I love Cajun food, especially gumbo and crawfish boils. I used to be on a gymnastics team and in Girl Scouts, but after a flare-up and a fall, I'm not currently doing either one. I'm a good student and math is my best subject. Not because it's interesting, but because it's easy for me. My dog Chloe died, and I was sad for a long time, but now I have Charlie, who gives the best doggy kisses in the world. Nobody can really tell I have FOP yet except I can't raise my left arm much higher than my*

waist. I worry all the time about other people find-
ing out and treating me differently.

I hope you'll write back and tell me all about
you.

Your friend,

Kate

Dear Kate,

I am married and my husband's name is Matt.
In addition to our dogs, we have two cats, and
though I don't have any biological children, I enjoy
being a stepmother to Matt's kids from a previous
marriage. Like you, I have a brother. Kurt is older
than me, and I consider him my best friend. I have
a lot of hobbies. I like playing around with make-
up and I'm pretty crafty. I just finished making a
bookmark of a red bird and decorating it with sil-
ver beads and a purple tassel.

You mentioned being afraid that your friends
will treat you differently. I have found that some-
times people don't know how to treat me. Like I'll
be out with Matt and because I'm in a wheelchair,
people will address their comments to Matt as if
I'm incapable of understanding. Matt just stands
there and waits for me to speak up, and when I do,

that usually changes things. So . . . my advice for you is to stand up for yourself and let your friends know what you can still do. Don't run and hide. Most people I know with FOP are great problem solvers because we have to be. Almost every problem has a solution if you're creative enough.

Your friend,

Amie

PS. Since you mentioned Say Yes to the Dress, *I'll look through my pictures and send you one of me in my wedding dress.*

KATE, MEET HARPER

On my first day back at school, Dad offered to drive Chris and me there. His eyes met mine in the rearview mirror. "Nervous?"

"No, I'm good." I was actually looking forward to being back in school, but a little worried about lunch. I wasn't sure whether to plop down beside Nat and act like nothing had happened or take the easy way out and eat in the library. Both Nat and Jayla had texted after my fall to make sure I was okay, but I hadn't heard from Claire. I guessed she was either embarrassed by her mom's behavior or maybe she felt the same way?

"Last night was fun," Chris said. He and Izaak had taught me to play a retro *Star Wars* game.

"Yeah, it was." I got that warm, mushy feeling I sometimes had about my goofball brother.

Gaming had never really interested me. I'd always preferred something more active like gymnastics, or bouncing on the trampoline. But gaming was a lot more fun than staring at the ceiling.

"Start with the new player tutorial and create a character," Chris had said.

I'd created Brimira, a spell caster and healer. Stepping inside her shoes was an escape. It reminded me of reading a good book and imagining I was the protagonist.

Izaak was waiting by my locker. "What's up, Bean?"

A big smile spread across my face because Izaak was acting the same as always. He and Mindy were the only two of my friends not weirded out by FOP. "Not much."

"Brimira is pretty cool," he said. "I'm glad Chris talked you into playing with us."

"Thanks. Driving the speeder is my favorite part."

"Mine too. I wish those hovering motorcycles were actually real. All caught up with algebra homework?"

"Of course. Are you?"

Izaak ducked his head. "Nah, I need a tutor."

"A tutor? I'm already helping Chris. Want to study with us?"

"Sure. That'd be awesome."

I realized Mom was right: If I focused on the things I could still do—like math, and my newfound interest in video games—I'd probably be a lot happier.

I decided to be brave at lunch. Only it wasn't just the four of us at our usual table. "Kate, meet Harper," Claire said. "She's new and just joined the gymnastics team."

It seemed I'd been replaced. Harper had shoulder-length red hair, brown eyes, and a dusting of freckles across her nose. She was pretty *and* on the gymnastics team. I wished she'd move back to wherever she came from.

"I miss New Orleans," Harper said, "but making friends through gymnastics helps, and I'm excited there's room for me in the Girl Scout troop."

Nat gasped at the mention of Girl Scouts. Both Claire and Jayla looked down at their sandwiches.

My face overheated, like I'd just finished a tumbling run, and I vomited words without thinking. "My friend Mindy and I are individually registered Girl Scouts. We're not part of a troop, but we're working on badges and my mom is taking us on a swamp tour."

"I'm glad things worked out," Claire said softly.

I wondered if she was sorry her mom had kicked me out of the troop. Maybe I had misjudged her. But even if that was true, Mrs. Chevalier's attitude affected our friendship. And I'd just lied to Claire. I hadn't asked Mindy yet about going on a swamp tour.

It had been much easier to lie than to have my friends pity me even more.

IF I COULD CHANGE THE WORLD

When I got home from school, Amie had sent pictures: one of Charlyze and Lilybet, and another of her wedding day! Amie was sitting in her wheelchair, wearing a white satin dress and a veil appliqued with flowers. She had on just the right amount of blush and mascara; her long brown hair hung in soft curls. She looked beautiful, but even better, she looked . . . happy.

Mom had told me I could still have a bright future with FOP, but I'd worried she was just trying to make me feel better. Seeing Amie in her wedding gown made it seem entirely possible.

Dear Amie,

I love your wedding picture. You look so happy. Just like the brides in Say Yes to the Dress. *Have you ever watched the show? It even has a YouTube channel. Sometimes the moms and daughters don't agree about the dresses, and there's even one episode where the bride's wedding theme was skulls and roses. Did your wedding have a theme? Anyway, I would love to hear all about it.*

Xoxo,

Kate

Dear Kate,

Our wedding didn't have a theme, but because Matt is a HUGE Star Wars fan, I surprised him with a groom's cake that had a picture of Darth Vader. My wedding colors were red and white, and I carried roses of both colors mixed in with baby's breath. Because of FOP, I had to get creative with my wedding dress. It was made of white satin, but in two pieces, because that made it easier to put on, and I felt beautiful in it. I had a cosmetologist apply my makeup and style my hair, which was really fun. Probably my favorite part of the wedding was spending time with all our guests at the recep-

tion. It was the last time I ever saw my grandpa because he died not long afterwards, and I am so happy he got to attend my wedding.

Xoxo,

Amie

Dear Amie,

I loved hearing about your wedding. I understand about your grandpa because I adore both of my grandparents. They live in West Virginia, and I really wish they lived closer.

I have to write a paper for English class called "If I Could Change the World." I'm not really sure what to write about. My librarian said if she could change the world, she'd make it a more equitable place for Black people. If you could change the world, what would you do?

Xoxo,

Kate

Hi Kate,

Hmmm. If I could change the world. Since receiving your message, I've given that question a lot of thought. If I could change the world, I'd make life easier for people with disabilities. The newest motorized wheelchairs can go over curbs, through gravel, up stairs, and even raise to reach things, but the starting price is well over twenty thousand dollars. While I was lucky and Medicaid paid for my chair, at first my claim was denied, and I had to spend time and emotional energy to get it covered.

And a wheelchair is just the beginning. I also use a wheelchair-accessible van, and having it converted to fit my needs was expensive, and that wasn't covered by insurance at all. Housing is another problem. Houses are not usually built handicapped accessible and to make them so can cost tens of thousands of dollars.

I love shopping and going out to dinner, but both can be a big hassle due to lack of parking. When Matt and I can't find handicapped parking, we try to find two empty spots side by side. We park in one and use the other to let the ramp down so there's room to get my chair out. Once we've parked, tight doorways and crowded aisles can make it difficult for me to navigate. One positive thing is the recent addition of family or unisex bathrooms. Though this change was for transgender people, it also benefitted the disabled community since caregivers are not necessarily the same sex as the person they are caring for.

I'm sure I've told you more than you'd ever want to know, but I'm pretty passionate about disability rights. If you haven't read it, I would recommend Being Heumann: An Unrepentant Memoir of a Disability Rights Activist *by Judith Heumann and Kristen Joiner. Judith is in a wheelchair due to polio and has spent her life fighting for disability rights. She's one of my heroes.*

Xoxo,

Amie

I read Amie's message again and again, pretty sure I'd found my topic: disability rights. Now all I had to do was get it approved by Mrs. Landry, and then check with Ms. Batiste about *Being Heumann*. Since it wasn't a kid's book, she'd probably have to get it through interlibrary loan.

I was excited about finding a topic . . . until I remembered Girl Scouts. Ugh. Writing an English paper would be easy compared to earning my Public Speaker badge. I couldn't do it. Disability rights was way too personal. I didn't have the courage to tell my classmates about FOP.

No way.

UNDERNEATH THE STARS

Judith Heumann's book meant a lot to me. When she was growing up, kids who used wheelchairs were not allowed to attend school. Her parents didn't give up, though, and she was finally allowed to attend in fourth grade.

Being Heumann was the kind of story that made me want to write in the margins and highlight entire paragraphs, but the book didn't belong to me. It belonged to the library.

On Saturday morning I hurried into the kitchen, clutching the book to my chest. I could smell pancakes and bacon. "Mom, I need my own copy of this memoir. Can I order one from Cottonwood Books?"

Mom spooned pancake batter onto the griddle. "What's it about?"

That was a hard question. The book was Judith Heumann's memoir, but it was more than that. It was everybody's story who had ever become disabled by an accident, an illness, or even just being born with one. "It's about believing in yourself," I answered. "She says having a disability pushed her to work harder and achieve more."

Mom studied my face as if she could see through the skin and bones to all the emotions churning inside my brain. "That's impressive."

I thumbed through the book and stopped at my favorite passage. "'If you were to acquire a disability tomorrow, it would be a change. But I can tell you this: It wouldn't have to be a tragedy.'"

Mom's eyes were swimming with tears. "Ah, Bean, you're making me proud and I'm about to cry."

"So, does that mean I can use your credit card?"

"Yes," Mom said. "It surely does."

The following weekend Mindy and I floated in huge inflatable rafts underneath a jet-black sky. I had invited her over to work on our Girl Scout badges, but I was procrastinating.

"I love looking at the stars from your pool even better than through a telescope," Mindy said.

It was kind of perfect—a warm fall night and a heated pool. "How's Mateo?"

"Still competing against me for first chair, but so far I've been able to hold him off."

I scooted into a more upright position to take pressure off my back. "Hey, Mindy, do you think I should start wearing a T-shirt over my bathing suit?" I was worried about the new bone growth that stuck out from my shoulder blade like a tiny angel's wing.

Mindy shook her head. "You're fine. I don't think anybody would really notice, and besides your hair covers it."

I closed my eyes, listening to the crickets chirp. It had been an odd couple of weeks at school. I often felt more grown-up than the rest of the kids around me. While they chattered about homework and sports, I read *Being Heumann* and thought about courage.

"Earth to Kate," Mindy said. "What are you thinking about?"

"School."

"Are you still having lunch with the girls from gymnastics?"

I made quiet circles in the water, not meeting her

gaze. "Sometimes." A couple of days a week, I still had lunch with Claire, Nat, Jayla, and Harper, but I really preferred hanging out in the library. Ms. Batiste understood that I was struggling. She had listened when I'd read passages of *Being Heumann* out loud.

"Kate," she'd said, "*you* have the heart and intelligence to achieve great things too." I had started to believe her. Maybe there was more than one way to become a champion.

And today, while I'd been reading, I'd made a connection between Judith Heumann and Jennifer Keelan, the little girl in the picture book Jayla had brought to my last Girl Scouts' meeting. Judith had written about the Capitol Crawl, and how Jennifer had climbed the steps of the Capitol building to show how hard it is for disabled people to enter lots of public buildings. I wanted to talk to Jayla about both books. We didn't have gymnastics in common anymore, but maybe it would give us something else to discuss.

These days it was hard for me to focus on anything besides having FOP. Maybe it was time to stop procrastinating and write about it. "Ready to work on our badges?"

Mindy rolled off her float into the warm water. "Sure, but can we have a snack first?"

"Of course. What's a sleepover without snacks? Let's grab M&M'S and take them to my room. I finally figured out what I want to say in my paper."

Mindy stopped treading water and grabbed the side of the pool. "Awesome. Are you going to read it in front of your English class?"

"Maybe. I haven't asked Mrs. Landry yet."

"She'll say yes," Mindy said. "Teachers love it when we volunteer to do extra work."

Once I opened my laptop, the words flowed across my screen. I didn't even need Chris's help. Amie and Judith Heumann had both inspired me to be brave, to speak up.

It turned out, I wasn't a chicken after all.

JAYLA

I scheduled my first tutoring session with Chris and Izaak for Sunday afternoon. "Izaak's bringing a bathing suit so we can go for a swim afterwards," Chris said.

I was flipping through TV channels, but nothing was worth watching. "I'll do homework so you and Izaak can have the pool."

Chris turned to face me on the sofa. "I already told Izaak we can't push you in or dunk you."

My breath came out in a relieved swoosh. Chris had understood without me saying a word. "Thanks." Sometimes I got tired of being different, of answering everybody's questions about FOP. "I'm glad you explained things to him."

Next I sent Jayla a text:

Izaak is coming over to study. Could I borrow that book you were reading: All the Way to the Top?

Sure. Heard you have a pool, btw.

Yeah, want to come over with Izaak?

I would love to.

"Why are you smiling?" Chris asked.

"I don't know. I'm just in a good mood." What I didn't say was that if Jayla had a good time today, maybe we could be real friends again.

"Bean, you're a genius," Izaak said.

Chris groaned. "Man, don't tell her that."

I was helping both boys correct our last algebra quiz.

"I'm *not* a math genius," I said, "but I did pay attention when Ms. Smith explained about removing the parentheses."

"Paying attention always helps," Jayla said with a giggle. She was cuddling on the sofa with Charlie. "This is the cutest dog I've ever seen."

Charlie usually ignored people who weren't part of our family, but he'd made an exception for Jayla.

Things seemed almost back to normal. When Jayla had given me the book, she'd said, "We can still work on our Girl Scouts badges together sometimes, even if we're not in the same troop."

Having FOP was like a roller coaster ride that never ends. Today I was up, but last night I had dreamed about nailing my bars routine at regionals. The dream had been so real I'd actually felt my body spinning through the air. I'd woken up and come crashing down. I'd never be able to do another bars routine.

"Hey, can you go over that thing about the parentheses again?" Izaak asked. "The last problem is kicking my tail."

I was trying to focus on the things I could still do, but sometimes it didn't work.

After a swim, Jayla and I relaxed in lounge chairs, while Chris and Izaak played water volleyball. "You can join them if you want to. I don't mind."

Jayla shook her head. "No, I'd rather be with you."

Then she asked, "So why did you want to borrow my book?"

I explained about Judith Heumann and how she had written about the Capitol Crawl.

While Jayla listened, her warm brown eyes reminded me of a time before FOP, a time when friendships had been easier.

"I felt awful when you fell at our Girl Scouts' meeting," she said, "and I feel guilty hanging out with Harper. I know you have lunch alone in the library sometimes."

I pulled the towel tight to give myself a hug. "It's hard for all of us, I guess. I can't expect the four of you not to talk about gymnastics, but I feel left out when you do." I thought about my bad dream again and how I'd never be able to compete. But what I missed most was how the gymnastics team had been like a second family. Without it, I felt lost.

Jayla watched the boys smack the volleyball back and forth over the net. "For most of fifth grade I had lunch in the library."

Fifth grade was before we moved to Baton Rouge and Jayla had never told me that before. "Why?"

"Because I'm one of the few Black kids. But then I

got to know Claire at gymnastics and started having lunch with her."

That explained why Jayla was loyal to Claire, even when Claire was acting bossy. "Having lunch in the library isn't so bad. Ms. Batiste is awesome," I said.

"Ms. Batiste is better than awesome. She told me she'd miss me when I started having lunch with Claire and Nat, but she was really happy I'd made some friends."

Nat—I missed *her* too. But she had always been so active—hiking, climbing the rock wall at the Y, and kicking the soccer ball around. I wasn't sure how to be friends with her now that I had FOP.

"I talked to my mom about us," Jayla told me. "She said it's bound to be awkward at first, but we just have to keep on being friends until it isn't awkward anymore."

"You really think we can be friends the way we used to?"

Jayla rolled her eyes. "Of course I do. Who else do you know that's as much fun as me?"

I smiled so big it felt like my face might split in two. We were back to kidding around instead of Jayla acting as if I were dying. "*Nobody* is as much fun as you.

And nobody makes better sugar cookies than *me*."

"Very true," Jayla said. "Want to make some now? Our brothers will be hungry when they finally get out of the water."

"Sure, let's do it!"

Jayla and I changed back into our clothes, then I rummaged in the junk drawer for cookie cutters shaped like jack-o'-lanterns, bats, and ghosts.

"Ooh, I love Halloween," Jayla said. "I still haven't decided about my costume, though. Have you?"

"No, not yet." I hadn't given Halloween much thought, but it wouldn't be the same as last year.

HALLOWEEN

Last year, I'd trick-or-treated with Claire, Nat, and Jayla, but this year walking around in the dark didn't seem like such a good idea. What if I tripped and fell? I was afraid to go, and felt really sorry for myself.

I reached for my phone and thumbed through Amie's messages. One sentence stuck out: *Because of FOP, I had to get creative with my wedding dress.* Creative—now that was a fun word. It somersaulted in my mind. Amie hadn't let FOP ruin her day. She couldn't wear a traditional wedding dress so she had found an alternative solution. I needed an alternative solution to Halloween—a way to see all my friends without stumbling around in the dark. I had an idea, but I'd need lots of help.

Dear Amie,

Thank you for being my friend and for being so awesome! Your messages helped me solve two problems.

I read Judith Heumann's book and wrote my English paper about disability rights.

What you said about getting creative inspired me to plan a Halloween open house for my friends. I'm baking sugar cookies shaped like bats, ghosts, pumpkins, and vampires, and making green punch. I found this cool mold so I can freeze water in the shape of a bony hand, which I think will look really creepy floating in the punch.

Do you have any plans for Halloween?

Xoxo,

Kate

Amie sent back a picture of herself dressed as a vampire. Her hair had been slicked back, her eyebrows darkened, her skin powdered to look really pale, and best of all, she had fangs.

Hi Kate,

I'm glad you wrote your English paper about disability rights. Way to go!

Here is a picture of my costume from last year, but I'm planning to wear it again this year. I'll be handing out treats to all the ghosts and goblins.

Xoxo,

Amie

Dad and Chris stretched netting across the bushes in front of our house to create a web and placed a huge spider in the center of it. They hung two skeletons from a tall oak tree dripping with Spanish moss.

While Dad and Chris were busy on the outside, Mom, Mindy, and I decorated inside, and then started baking.

Inhaling, Mindy closed her eyes. "The mummy dogs smell awesome, like fresh-baked bread."

Not only did they smell good, but they had been really easy to make. We had cut crescent dough into thin strips and wrapped it like bandages around hot dogs.

Next, Mindy and I spread a black cloth across the dining room table; we set out orange napkins and paper plates. Mom filled the punch bowl because she didn't trust us not to spill it. "Girls, you did a great job icing the cookies," she said. "As good as a bakery."

At 6:00, with the song "Monster Mash" blaring from the speakers, the doorbell rang, and I rushed to answer it. It was Claire. It was the first time we'd seen each other outside of school since I'd fallen at Girl Scouts and our moms had argued.

Claire had turned herself into a beautiful ballerina, with her hair swept up into a bun and a sparkling tiara. "Hi. Great costume," she said.

I had copied Amie and dressed as a vampire. "Thanks. Come on in."

A few minutes later, Nat arrived wearing a team USA soccer jersey with the number 15 on the back. Best of all, she had dyed her hair pink. "Hey, it's Megan Rapinoe!" I said.

Nat grinned. "Like my hair? I already had the same haircut as Megan. I wanted to dye it, but Mom insisted on a spray that will wash out."

"It's really cool. How about some punch and cookies?"

Izaak and Jayla arrived next. Izaak was dressed in a tuxedo, a bow tie, and carrying a trumpet. He looked debonair (a recent vocabulary word). "Louis Armstrong?" I guessed.

A wide smile stretched across his face. "Exactly right, Bean! I considered dressing up like Steve Irwin, but too much khaki."

Jayla wore a purple satin evening gown with sequins shaped like stars on the skirt. She looked amazing, but I didn't know who she was supposed to be. "Ella Fitzgerald," she said. "I copied this dress from a book about her."

"It's beautiful. Did you make it yourself?"

Jayla shook her head. "No, Mom helped me."

Mindy was leaning against the wall in our dining room, facing Chris. She had dressed as an astronaut in an orange jumpsuit but had ditched her helmet. Chris was decked out as the Phantom of the Opera. He was such a ham. I just knew he was waiting for an opportunity to sing.

I pulled out my phone and took pictures:

The mummy dogs,

the cookies,

the green punch,

and all my friends.

I'd send pictures to Amie and never forget this party.

Mom brought out a fresh tray of mummy dogs. "Having fun, Bean?"

I nodded. It wasn't my usual Halloween. It wasn't the Halloween I would have chosen. But . . . it was still wonderful.

A STANDING 0

I talked to Mrs. Landry and asked if I could read my paper to our English class. She loved the idea, but I was worried. Not about giving a speech, but about telling my classmates about FOP. Would it be like the time I had burped really loud in third grade? Everyone had stared at me, appalled.

"Class, Kate Lovejoy has written an exceptional English paper, one she'd like to read out loud to meet the requirements for her Public Speaker badge in Girl Scouts. Please face forward and listen to her."

I smiled at my classmates to sort of break the ice, and Izaak winked at me to calm me down. I took a deep breath, saying a silent prayer to St. Sebastian.

If I Could Change the World by Kate Lovejoy

If I could change the world, I'd make life easier for people with disabilities. I had never given that much thought until I was diagnosed with Fibrodysplasia Ossificans Progressiva (FOP). FOP is a rare genetic disorder that makes your body grow an extra skeleton. Right now, I have extra bone in my shoulder, and any kind of accident or injury could cause my body to grow even more bone in places where it's not supposed to.

Since my diagnosis, I have been corresponding with a woman who has the same disease as I do. Because Amie is older, her disease has progressed further than mine. Amie is in a wheelchair.

Amie shared with me some problems that are common among disabled people. Did you know that a motorized wheelchair can cost over twenty thousand dollars? Or that to make a house handicapped accessible can cost even more?

Most of us take things like going shopping or out to eat for granted, but both can be a big challenge for Amie. Sometimes all the handicapped spots are taken and her husband can't find room to park their van and let the ramp down. And even after they find parking, narrow doorways and crowded aisles make it hard for Amie to get around.

I wish I could change all of that. Not only for Amie, but for everyone who uses a wheelchair. Since I can't, I was feeling pretty hopeless, until my mom told me about the Serenity Prayer. It goes like this:

God grant me the serenity
To accept the things
I cannot change;
The courage to change the things I can;
And the wisdom to know the difference.

So, no offense to Mrs. Landry, but maybe we've been looking at how to change the world all wrong. Maybe instead of focusing on big things that are too hard to accomplish alone, we should focus on things we can do, even if they only change the world a little bit.

FOP is classified as an orphan disease because so few people have it. FOP only affects one out of every two million people. Because orphan diseases are so rare, not enough money goes into research and treatment for them. One thing I can do to

change the world is help raise money for Dr. Fred
Kaplan's research lab at the University of Pennsyl-
vania Medical School.

If every student and faculty member at Five
Oaks Middle School donated one dollar, we could
raise a thousand dollars for FOP research. I have
permission to set up a collection jar in the office,
and I'll send all the donations to Dr. Fred.

Throughout the school year, I'm planning to
organize other fundraisers too, and I'm hoping
some of my classmates will join me. It will take a
miracle for Dr. Fred and his team to find a cure,
and I need everyone's help.

At first the room was so quiet I wanted to run and
hide, but then my classmates started clapping. Loud.
Jayla stood up first, and then Izaak, Nat, and even
Claire, and then everybody else. It was . . . a standing
ovation!

"Excellent!" Mrs. Landry said. "I hope you'll consider
reading your paper at a school-wide assembly."

I gulped. *School-wide?* I knew all the kids in my
class, but I didn't know everyone at my school. Speaking at an assembly terrified me. I took a breath as deep

as the ocean before answering her. "Maybe. I need to think about it."

Several of my classmates raised their hands. They had a lot of questions about FOP, and thanks to the handbook, I had a lot of answers. I only stumbled once. It happened when Peter, a boy I didn't know very well, asked me a question. "Will you need a wheelchair like Amie?"

I looked up at the ceiling, and then down at the floor. "I don't know for sure. Not even the doctors do. FOP affects everybody differently."

"That stinks," he said. "I'll donate my allowance."

I had made a new friend.

Dear Amie,

I did it! I presented my paper in class and earned my Public Speaker badge in Girl Scouts. I'm including a photo for you to see. But now I have an even bigger challenge. My teacher Mrs. Landry wants me to read the paper at a school-wide assembly. I'm not sure I'm brave enough to tell that many people about FOP. HELP!

Xoxo,

Kate

CHRIS

During lunch, I sent Mom a text:

Mrs. Landry loved my speech!

Proud of you, Bean!

She wants me to speak in front of the entire school.

Wow! That calls for a celebration.

Can we do takeout? Gumbo from Roux's???

Sure, I'll pick some up.

• • •

My mouth watered as Mom served the spicy gumbo. "Bean, I'm so proud of you. Being asked to speak in front of the entire school is really impressive."

"I *sing* in front of large audiences all the time," Chris said.

Mom and Dad exchanged worried looks. Finally, Dad said, "This isn't a competition. We're proud of both of you."

Chris looked down at his gumbo.

I hated to admit it, but in a way we *were* competing, and Chris had no way of winning. Since my diagnosis, Dad had spent a lot of time researching FOP in the LSU library and corresponding with Dr. Fred's team. Mom had overseen construction of the pool, had workmen add a grab bar in the shower, and had taken up all the rugs because she was afraid I'd trip over them.

"I'm always proud you're my brother, Chris. You have an amazing voice," I said.

Chris's jaw relaxed and he took another bite of gumbo.

"There's a convention coming up for FOP families," Dad said. "It's in Orlando. I thought we could combine it with a trip to Disney World."

A huge smile spread across Chris's face, the kind

usually reserved for Broadway musicals. "Can we include the Harry Potter park at Universal Studios?"

"I don't see why not," Dad said.

We had gone to Disney once before, after a close friend of Mom's died in a car accident. In one of the photos, Mom is riding on the carousel. She's smiling, but her eyes are red from crying. "We went to Disney seven years ago, after Robin died," I said.

Mom got a faraway look in her eyes. "We sure did. My heart was broken, but being there helped. I'm looking forward to going back."

Dad leaned toward Chris. "The convention organizers recognize that FOP affects the whole family. There will be workshops for parents and siblings too."

"Do they teach you how to deal with pain-in-the-butt little sisters?" Chris joked.

"I am not a pain in the butt!" I said indignantly, but then I giggled, because sometimes I could be. I stuck my tongue out at Chris. "You're a pain in the butt too."

Mom and Dad broke out laughing. "Maybe they'll have some tips for both of you," Dad said.

Mom pushed her chair back and stood up. "Chris and Bean, I could use some help clearing the table. Afterwards, we'll have dessert and presents."

"What kind of presents?" I asked.

"I'm more interested in the bread pudding," Chris said. "I saw it in the kitchen."

"Aha," Mom said. "Now I know who snuck a spoonful!"

PRAYER QUILTS

Mom had said presents, but there was only one box, addressed in Grandma's handwriting to both Chris and me.

Chris peeled the tape away, then ripped open the box. All we could see was bubble wrap.

"Wonder what's underneath," I said.

"Only one way to find out," Chris said, and started unwinding the bubble wrap. Finally, we could see two bundles—quilts. Each quilt had an envelope pinned to it. My quilt was made of burgundy- and cream-colored squares, while Chris's was just like it, except his was cream and blue.

Chris handed me the envelope with my name on it. I couldn't wait and ripped into it.

Dear Bean,

As each knot is tied in a prayer quilt, a prayer is offered for the person who will receive the quilt. If you'll count the knots, you'll see that I prayed for you over a hundred times. I don't understand much about FOP, but I do know that prayer can help you get through most dark days. I hope this quilt keeps you warm and reminds you of how proud I am of you.

Love,

Grandma

I ran my fingers across the knots, imagining my grandma saying all those prayers for me. Chris blinked back tears. "My allergies are acting up."

He did have terrible allergies, but I didn't think they were what was making him cry. "What did your letter say?" I asked.

Chris shook his head. "I'd rather keep it private, but Grandma has prayed for me over a hundred times."

"Let's take a picture with the quilts," Mom said. "A picture will make your grandma smile."

*   *   *

Mom helped me spread the prayer quilt on my bed. I snuggled underneath it, checking messages. Amie had replied to me.

Dear Kate,

I'm not surprised your speech went so well because it flowed from your heart. The best writing and speaking usually do. I have no doubt you are brave enough to present at a school-wide assembly. Just remember, your family is already proud of you, and I am too. I've done some public speaking myself and I have a couple of tips:

1. Remember to smile at the audience, and

2. read slowly.

My final piece of advice is a Christopher Robin quote: "You are braver than you believe, stronger than you seem, and smarter than you think."

Xoxo,

Amie

I read Amie's message through a couple of times and then stared at my blank walls. I could still see the faint outlines of the posters of Simone, Aly, and Gabby that used to hang there. I read the Christopher Robin quote a third time. If I could find a poster of it, the quote would cover one of the shadows. Eventually, I'd replace the other shadows too.

Dear Amie,

In one of your earlier messages, you mentioned having a brother. How did your having FOP affect him? I think Chris is struggling. I guess we should talk about it, but I don't know what to say. And tonight, Dad offered to take us to the FOP convention in Orlando. Will you be there? I would love to meet you.

Xoxo,

Kate

Dear Kate,

My brother, Kurt, was overprotective of me, and when he was younger wanted to work with Dr. Fred and "fix me." I think he also grew into a bit of a loner and kept his problems to himself because he had average middle school problems, and I had all of those plus FOP.

Yes, I am planning to attend the FOP convention

in Orlando and meeting you would be a real high-
light for me. The workshops for siblings helped my
brother, and I'll bet they would help yours too.

  Xoxo,
  Amie

KATE THE GREAT

The theme of our school-wide assembly was *Making a Difference*. Izaak pointed to a poster taped up by our lockers. "Bean, you're gonna be famous!"

"Stop it. I'm nervous enough already." The school had booked a presenter who was an artist/motivational speaker, and then I'd follow him. Mrs. Landry had practiced with me every day after school.

"Your adoring fans are waiting," Izaak teased.

"You really are making me nervous."

The smile slid from his face, which almost never happened. "Sorry. I didn't mean to. I was just kidding around."

"It's okay." I nudged him with my elbow. "Just promise to clap for me, even if I mess up."

I sat in the front row between our guest speaker, who had a shiny, bald head, and our principal, Mr. Connick, who tried to hide his bald spot by combing his hair across it. He rose and welcomed the student body. " I believe every one of you has the potential to change the world for the better."

I looked down at my notecards, remembering Amie's advice. Smile and read slowly. I wished I'd been scheduled first, to get it over with, but instead I'd have to wait.

"We have a special guest with us here today," Mr. Connick continued. "One who has spoken before thousands of schoolchildren. Robert Snyder will entertain us, motivate us, and inspire us with his storytelling and his art, and then one of our very own students, Miss Kate Lovejoy, will challenge us to raise money for a cause close to her heart. Take it away, Robert!"

Mr. Snyder stood in front of a large black canvas. The lights dimmed, then symphony music soared. He started with the story of Helen Keller and talked about how an illness had left her blind and deaf. Mr. Snyder drew the entire time he was speaking. I watched as a life-sized picture began to emerge from his colored chalks.

"Wow," I whispered.

Mr. Connick turned and smiled. "He's impressive, right?"

I forgot to be nervous as Mr. Snyder's voice swept me away to 1915. Helen had co-founded an organization to help soldiers blinded during WWI. "Who better to help blind soldiers," Mr. Snyder asked, "than a woman who'd lived with the challenges of blindness herself?"

I wiped away tears and was glad the auditorium had been darkened. Helen's story was my story too—finding courage when faced with a disability. Helen was a hero—my new definition of a champion.

Mr. Snyder stepped away from the canvas. "Ladies and gentlemen, I present to you a portrait of Helen Keller!"

The applause sounded like thunder. My presentation was bound be a big, boring letdown.

Finally, it was my turn. I stood on shaky legs, then climbed the steps to the podium. I gazed out at a sea of my classmates, all dressed in the navy shirts we wore. "Wow, Mr. Snyder was terrific," I said. "How would you like to speak after *him?*"

The other kids laughed, which gave me the confidence to keep going. I remembered what Amie said and spoke from my heart. I recited my notes about FOP and the steep odds of finding a cure, but then from somewhere deep inside I found the courage to ad-lib. "If Helen Keller hadn't been deaf and blind, she probably wouldn't have founded the organization to help soldiers, and if I didn't have FOP, I wouldn't be standing here today to raise money and awareness for it. I know you can help me do it. Thank you."

Mr. Snyder was the first person on his feet. In a matter of seconds every student and teacher was standing too. "We can do this!" he roared. "Let's defeat FOP!"

I felt invincible. I loved his words even more than the applause that accompanied them. In that moment, defeating FOP seemed not only possible but inevitable. I was a superhero—Kate the Great!

But that feeling wouldn't last.

THE IFOPA CONVENTION

Our hotel had a courtyard inside of it with ponds, trees, and walkways. The guestrooms were located in a circle, with the exhibit hall in the middle. After we unpacked, Mom and Dad left to find the business center so they could check in for the conference and pick up our nametags and itinerary.

Chris stretched across one of the beds, then thumbed through a Disney brochure. "Are you looking forward to the conference, or nervous about it?"

"Both." I leaned back in an armchair and put my feet up on a stool. After we had agreed to attend the conference, Mom had had second thoughts. She worried that seeing how the disease had progressed in some of the older attendees might be too upsetting for me. Dad was still in favor. He wanted to attend a workshop on gene therapy research and have Dr. Fred examine me.

"If the conference is going to make Kate sad, maybe we should skip it and head to Disney World and Universal," Chris had said the night we all discussed it.

Finally, Dad had turned to me. "It's up to you, Bean."

I've always been brave about medical stuff. Watched when nurses had drawn my blood or given me a shot. And besides, I wanted to meet Amie. "Let's go to the conference," I'd said. "I'll be fine."

I took a long time getting ready in our hotel room because I wanted to make a good first impression on Amie. Since I'd lost some mobility in my left arm, styling my hair was hard for me. I usually insisted on doing it myself, but that day, I let Mom use the curling wand to give my hair beachy waves.

Amie and her husband, Matt, were waiting for us in the lobby. I recognized them right away from their wedding pictures. "Amie, it's me, Kate!"

She hurried to meet me in her motorized wheelchair, then clasped my hand and gave it a gentle squeeze. "I look forward to your messages every day, Kate."

I squeezed her hand back. It was like meeting Mindy at space camp. Finding another best friend was as rare as a perfect moonrock.

Dinner was in a banquet hall. Mom and Dad mingled with the parents of other FOP kids, while Chris and Matt bonded over their love of video games. Dr. Chen had been right about FOP affecting everyone differently. Some people used canes, some walkers, some wheelchairs. I saw a woman with her arms permanently crossed like an X and a boy who couldn't raise his head.

"It's hard not to stare, isn't it?" Amie asked.

"Yes. I've only seen pictures online."

"The woman with her arms crossed is Jeannie Peeper. She founded the International FOP Association. We're all connected because of her."

"I told Mom I could handle being here, but I'm . . . I'm overwhelmed."

"Then let's change the subject," Amie said. "Here's something I haven't told you. Being your mentor has helped me. It makes me feel better about having FOP."

"That's a relief. Since I'm younger, sometimes I worry about being a pest!"

Amie shook her head. "Don't ever worry about that.

Our friendship is reciprocal," she said. "And by the way, your hair looks so pretty."

"Thanks. Mom styled it for me."

Amie stared into my eyes. "I gave you a compliment. Why are you scowling?"

"Because I probably couldn't have fixed my hair this way on my own," I said.

"There are lots of things I can't do on my own anymore," Amie said. "But one thing that helps is the Ability Toolbox Program. There's a workshop about it tomorrow morning. You should come!"

Mom and I attended the Ability Toolbox presentation together. We sat at a round table, listened to speakers, and watched a slideshow. I took notes in my journal. The first speaker was the mom of an FOP kid. "The goal of the Ability Toolbox Program is to help people with FOP lead more independent lives," she said.

Mom blinked back tears. She had taken a leave of absence from her job. I could still do most things for myself, but if my FOP got worse, she and Dad would have to spend more time helping me. I took some deep breaths to relax. It could be years before I had another flare-up, and besides, Dr. Fred and his team were searching for a cure.

The speaker pushed a strand of hair behind her ear and flipped to a slide that said:

Identify the limitation: e.g. reaching things, bending over to get something from the floor, toileting independently, eating without help

Look for a tool: Amazon, Google Search, social media

If no tool can be found, adapt one

I thought about the Woodworker badge in Girl Scouts. Maybe Grandpa could teach me to make a tool that would help people with FOP style their hair.

After the first speaker finished, another mom took her place behind the podium. "The best advice I have ever been given was that if I treated my son with FOP as capable, then he would be." I nudged Mom with my elbow.

The speaker said her son has a bed that elevates, with a fall pad beside it, just in case he rolls out of bed.

He uses a dressing stick to put his clothes on and a grabber to turn the lights off and on.

I discovered a whole world of tools that I hadn't even known existed.

Then I saw a dog—a service dog named Pine! He stood beside the third speaker's wheelchair. Pine was amazing: He could retrieve dropped items, carry grocery bags, and even tug doors open.

Pine's owner held a silver stick called a Scooper Genie. It allowed her to pick up dog poop without having to bend down. I copied the words *Scooper Genie* in my journal and drew a star by them.

The last speaker was a middle-aged man who had been living with FOP for a long time. I copied one of his quotes into my notebook. *My body is inflexible, but I keep my mind flexible.*

I hoped there would be a cure for FOP before I needed a wheelchair, or any of the other tools the speakers had mentioned. I said yet another silent prayer to St. Sebastian. He was probably tired of hearing from me.

DISNEY

Chris and I had always loved roller coasters. We dared each other to keep our eyes open. We never screamed going backward or upside down. The problem was I had lost my nerve. Every roller coaster came with risks. A hard bump could trigger a flare-up.

"How about Space Mountain?" Chris asked.

"Sure," I answered, but inside I felt anything *but* sure. We had a forty-five-minute wait, and I felt more anxious with every passing second.

"Dad can ride with Chris instead," Mom whispered. "Let's you and me grab an ice cream cone."

I shook my head. Space Mountain was pretty tame as far as roller coasters went. I wanted to brave it. And

I wanted to ride Expedition Everest and the Rock 'n' Roller Coaster too. Except what if I suffered a flare-up over something as unimportant as an amusement park ride?

Disney has lots of accommodations for people with disabilities. There's the Disability Access System for guests who have trouble standing in long lines. You can rent wheelchairs and electronic conveyance vehicles. They've planned for kids with hearing disabilities and kids on the autism spectrum. But none of those accommodations helped me. My problem was mental. I was scared. I hadn't figured out how to balance the things I used to enjoy with the changes in my body. I hadn't figured out how to live with FOP.

Chris got more and more excited. He bounced on the balls of his feet.

My pancakes churned in my stomach.

Mom and Dad were leaving roller coasters up to me. A part of me was glad. I had asked them not to make decisions without me, but having choices was hard too.

"Only fifteen minutes!" Chris said.

I wiped sweat off my forehead.

Mom squeezed my clammy hand.

I kept shuffling forward.

Finally, it was our turn. Chris climbed in and patted the empty seat beside him.

It felt like everyone was watching me, like the time I had refused to jump off the high dive at the pool.

I begged Chris with my eyes not to be mad. "Mom, could we leave Dad and Chris here and go to Epcot?"

Mom let out a relieved sigh. "Of course we can. Epcot is wonderful."

It was a hot day and the Mexico Pavilion was awesome. The painted sky looked more purple than black. There was a huge volcano smoldering in the background.

Mom pointed to the pyramid. "I think it's Mayan."

We shopped in the Mexican Folk Art Gallery while a mariachi band played. I bought some wooden maracas for Mindy, and then we took a boat ride.

"How about tacos for lunch?" I asked.

"Fine by me," Mom said, "but there are lots of other countries to see. Are you sure you wouldn't rather look around first?"

"I'm sure. Nothing beats tacos."

While we waited to be served, Mom reached out and patted my hand. "I'm proud of you. You found a way to enjoy yourself without spoiling Chris's fun."

I shrugged. "Chris is lucky. I'm still jealous."

"He *is* lucky," Mom said, "and don't beat yourself up over being human. If the situations were reversed, I'll bet Chris would feel the same way."

"Know what I was just thinking about?"

Mom shook her head. "Nope. Tell me."

"I was remembering the last time I took a roller coaster ride. I had no idea it would be the last. If I'd known, I would have enjoyed it more. I would have memorized every detail."

"That's the way life is," Mom said. "I don't remember the last time I carried you or Chris on my hip. I just know suddenly you were too big and I couldn't do it anymore."

"Do you think I should have ridden Space Mountain?"

Mom's dark brown eyes stared into mine. "I think it would have been okay," she finally said, "but I was relieved when you said no. There is no right answer. There's only the answer that feels right to you."

The waitress served my tacos and Mom's enchiladas. This day wasn't going according to plan, but I was determined to still have fun.

"Bean," Mom said, "sometimes the bravest people are the ones who just say no."

I wasn't sure I agreed, but I wanted to think about it a lot more.

CONNECTING WITH NAT

I didn't feel comfortable playing soccer or jumping on the trampoline, but I wanted to reconnect with Nat. As Ms. Smith scribbled X and Y equations on the whiteboard, I didn't pay much attention. Instead, I wondered whether Nat had decided which badge to work on in Girl Scouts—Trailblazing or Field Day?

Ms. Smith asked for a volunteer to solve the first equation, and I raised my hand to get it over with. "It's a Small World" played inside my head. Chris and I had both caught earworms, hearing that song ever since our trip to Disney.

"Nice job, Kate," Ms. Smith said. "Do I have a volunteer for the next equation? What about you, Izaak?"

Izaak hated being called on for math problems. I felt sorry for him, but went back to thinking about Nat.

Just then she glanced at me over her shoulder, as if she had sensed I was thinking about her. Suddenly I had an idea. What if Nat organized a Field Day to raise money for FOP research? She had to work on her Girl Scouts badge anyway, so it might as well be for a good cause. I hated asking her for a favor, though. Nat had barely called or texted since I'd told her about my FOP.

I thought about Nat for the rest of the school day. I almost asked her at lunch, but Harper and Claire didn't give me much of a chance. They spent the entire time talking about an upcoming gymnastics meet.

After school, I completely chickened out and decided to send Nat a text. A text had two advantages: 1. It would give Nat time to think about whether she really wanted to plan a field day, and 2. A text meant I didn't have to worry about my face turning red if she said no.

Hi Nat. I was wondering if you'd decided whether to work on the Trailblazer or Field Day badge? And if you're going for the Field Day one, maybe you'd consider calling it Field Day for FOP and helping me raise money for research?

I waited anxiously for an answer, but my phone didn't vibrate.

Not when I took Charlie for a walk.

Not while I finished my homework.

Not while I ate dinner.

After my shower, Chris knocked on my bedroom door. "Come on. Mom gave us an extra half hour to play video games."

I followed him to take my mind off waiting for Nat.

Five minutes before bedtime, my phone finally buzzed.

It was Nat calling.

A FIELD DAY FOR FOP

"**H**i, Nat," I answered, my heart pounding.

"Hi."

She didn't say anything else, just breathed into the phone.

"It's okay if you don't want to do it," I offered.

"What? Uh . . . no, that's not the problem. A Field Day for FOP is a great idea."

"Okay, then what *is* the problem?"

"I wanted to say I'm sorry for . . . you know, not being around much."

It was my turn to breathe into the phone. I thought of what one of the speakers had shared at the FOP conference: *Sometimes FOP makes me feel invisible. People don't really look at me, or talk to me, because they don't want to embarrass themselves by doing or saying the wrong thing.* "Apology accepted, but I've missed hanging out with you."

"I've missed you too," she said. "And I've been researching field days online. We'll need a *lot* of volunteers."

Nat decided our field day would be sort of like a carnival or state fair, so that kids who aren't athletic could still have fun. She invited the parent-teacher organization to participate, but Nat was the one in charge. She called our first meeting to order in the school auditorium. I looked around and counted seventy-five people in the audience. I was in awe that so many kids and their parents wanted to help. Mindy sat beside me. I had asked her to come, even though she didn't go to our school.

"Thank you for volunteering for the first annual Field Day for FOP," Nat said. "I think the best way to start is by assigning jobs. I'll need a couple of volunteers to grill hot dogs." She grinned. "And I would prefer adult volunteers because kids in charge of a hot grill doesn't seem like such a good idea."

"Hey," Izaak said. "Some kids are responsible."

Claire's mom raised her hand. "My husband and I will be in charge of refreshments, and I'll recruit some of my friends to handle fruit cups, lemonade, and iced tea."

Mom's eyes shot daggers at Mrs. Chevalier. She was still holding a grudge about Girl Scouts and had told me, "I can forgive almost anybody who hurts me, but mess with one of my kids and I have a hard time getting past it."

Nat nodded. "Thank you. That would be a big help."

I took notes as Nat assigned jobs. Izaak agreed to referee a dodge ball game; our PE teacher would handle volleyball. Claire offered to organize a Hula-Hoop marathon, and Jayla volunteered to make posters publicizing the event. Other volunteers signed up to be in charge of sack races, a dance station, face painting, and the most unique idea of all: throwing rolls of toilet paper through a toilet bowl lid. Chris was in charge of that one.

I raised my hand. "Mindy and I want to have a Frosting for FOP booth and sell iced cookies."

"Great idea," Nat said. "I need you to give a speech too. Tell everyone about FOP and why raising money for it is important."

I smiled. I had always considered math my superpower, but I was discovering new talents—writing and speaking.

Ms. Batiste raised her hand. "I have a friend who's a reporter for *The Advocate*. I'll call her and ask if she'll write an article about Kate and the field day."

"That would be awesome!" Nat said, pumping her fist in the air.

But Ms. Batiste didn't stop there. "We should have an information booth. I'll run it and hand out brochures about FOP."

"Kate's mom and I would like to help with that," Dad said. "We're just back from the FOP family gathering. I have lots of information on drug trials and promising new research."

"Great!" Nat said. "Thanks for a terrific first meeting. Let's meet again in two weeks to share updates."

Mindy squeezed my hand. Having close friends made hard things easier, and good things like tonight even better.

THE MANAGER

The Field Day for FOP wouldn't happen until the spring, but I discovered it takes months of planning to pull off a big event. Thanksgiving was just around the corner, and it seemed everyone was working on Field Day. Conversations at lunch were about Nat's efforts to keep the volunteers organized (which she compared to herding cats); Jayla often shared her poster designs; and Claire was convinced her Hula-Hoop marathon would be epic.

"Why didn't anybody include *me* in Field Day?" Harper asked at lunch one day, twirling the straw in her milk carton.

Nat shrugged her shoulders. "I didn't mean to

leave you out. Just jump in. What do you want to do?"

"Organize a gymnastics demonstration."

Nat winced, glancing over at me. "That's up to Kate."

I had been giving gymnastics a lot of thought. I missed it—missed being part of a team. "Sure," I said, "that would be great. You know, I've been thinking about talking to Coach Buchanan. Maybe I could become the manager of the team."

Real smiles spread across the faces of all my friends, and it was contagious. I smiled back, relieved that they liked the idea.

When I got home from school, Mom was in the kitchen making a chicken casserole. "I've invited Ms. Batiste over for dinner. We're going to design the brochures together."

"Good! I love Ms. Batiste." I pulled a chair up at the kitchen table and watched Mom mix ingredients.

"How was school today?" she asked.

"I had the best day I've had since the assembly."

Mom's smile lit up her whole face. "That's the kind of news I like to hear. What made it so special?"

"I talked to my friends about becoming the manager of the gymnastics team. Keeping track of permission slips and medical forms and going to all the meets to cheer them on."

Mom's lips trembled and she stopped stirring the casserole. "Bean, I'm about to cry, but for a happy reason. I'm so proud of you that I don't even know what to say."

I stood up, then hugged Mom from behind. "Don't cry. The casserole is soupy enough already."

Mom ran the back of her hand across her eyes. "I wish more than anything you didn't have FOP, but you have risen to the challenge."

I leaned my cheek against her shoulder. Some days I met the challenge, and some days I didn't. Some days I was sadder than sad. "Do I have time to make sugar cookies for dessert?"

"You sure do."

I rummaged in the junk drawer for a turkey cookie cutter. It seemed like the right choice because I'd had a good day. Turkeys always reminded me to be thankful.

FACE-FIRST

I was so tired during dinner, I was afraid of falling asleep and landing face-first in my chicken casserole. I kept fidgeting, hoping that would keep me awake, but then Chris leaned over and whispered, "Do you have ants in your pants?" I gave him the stink eye.

"I'm glad you're working with me," Mom said to Ms. Batiste. "I know a lot about FOP, but I've never designed a brochure before."

Ms. Batiste blotted her lips with a napkin. "I'm happy to help. Kate is one of my favorite students."

I tried to smile at that, but I had an awful headache; I just wanted the evening to be over with. When Mom brought my cookies out after dinner, I didn't even reach for one.

"Kate, aren't you having cookies?" Mom asked.

"Uh, no. Too full of chicken casserole." I left out that my throat felt sore. Something like ice cream would have gone down much better.

Chris piled a stack of cookies on his napkin. "Can I be excused? I still have a lot of homework."

Mom nodded. "Kate, would you like to be excused too? You look awfully tired."

"Yes, thank you. Ms. Batiste, I'm so glad you came over, but I've been about to fall asleep all evening."

As soon as I got to my room, I stretched across the bed, then pulled Grandma's prayer quilt up to my chin. I didn't have the energy left to change into my pajamas or to even brush my teeth. All I wanted was sleep.

My whole body ached. I had slept all night but still felt exhausted. My teeth chattered from the cold. I pulled Grandma's quilt over my head to try and get warm.

Mom knocked on the door. "Kate, want some pancakes?"

"Too sick," I mumbled.

She pushed the door open. "What? I couldn't hear you."

"I'm sick."

Mom rushed to my bedside. "Oh, Kate, you slept in

your clothes!" She reached out and placed her palm across my forehead. "You feel awfully warm. I'd better get the thermometer."

My temperature was 101. That number sent Mom scurrying for medication to reduce my fever. As I washed the pills down with water, my throat felt as rough as sandpaper.

Dad and Chris hovered in my bedroom doorway.

"Stay away. She's probably contagious," Mom said.

Dad's face scrunched into a worried frown. "The flu is going around my office. I think we should call Dr. Boudreaux and ask her to prescribe Tamiflu."

My parents had been debating the pros and cons of my getting the flu vaccine. The flu was dangerous for people with FOP, but so were injections. Doctors tried to minimize the risk by giving subcutaneous shots and smaller doses. I reached for Charlie, the best source of comfort I knew.

While Charlie stood guard, I slept all day. Mom woke me every few hours to sip warm broth and slept on the floor in my room.

On the second day, I dozed while the television played in the background. I was sick of broth, so we'd switched to Jell-O and ice pops.

I woke in the middle of the night to wet pajamas.

At first, I thought I had peed the bed, but my top was as damp as my bottoms. "Mom, Mom," I called.

She sprang out of her sleeping bag like a soldier ready for battle.

"Relax, Mom. I'm fine, just soaking wet."

Mom took my temperature. "Your fever has broken!"

The relief on her face felt almost as good as winning a gold medal.

"I'm planning to keep you out of school until Monday," Mom said. "You need to rest and build your strength up."

I took a good look at her. Mom's hair was greasy, she had dark circles under her eyes, and from the way she moved I could tell her back ached from sleeping on the floor. "You're the one who needs to rest," I told her.

"Don't worry about me," Mom said. "I'll be fine. There's nothing in the world more important than helping you avoid another flare-up."

"Hmmm. What would Grandma say?"

Mom shrugged. "That if I get sick, I can't take care of you."

"Exactly, Mom. It's way past your bedtime," I joked.

"I want you to eat something first."

I had leftover mashed potatoes and a strawberry milkshake. Nothing had ever tasted more delicious.

After a three-day snooze fest, I was wide awake. I messaged Amie.

Dear Amie,

Sorry I didn't answer you, but I've been sick with the flu. I'm still really tired, but as soon as I feel better, I'll send you a long description of the Field Day for FOP that my friend Nat is planning. I have to write another speech for it, but I don't really mind.

Xoxo,

Kate

Next, I answered texts from Mindy, Jayla, Nat, Claire, and Harper. I saved the one from Izaak for last.

Beanie Weanie, you're worrying me. Get well soon cause I need your help. Algebra and me don't mix.

I answered: *Dude, I'm happy to help. Maybe this weekend.*

It was only five thirty a.m. When my friends woke up, they'd know I was on the mend.

FERRIS BUELLER

We watched TV in the family room. Mom and Dad were both in great moods because the flu was behind me.

"I'm so relieved you're feeling better," Mom said.

Dad reached over and ruffled my hair. "This calls for a celebration. How about we do takeout? I could pick up po'boys."

Everybody had a favorite when it came to po'boy sandwiches. Mom wanted roast beef, Dad chose oysters, Chris decided on shrimp, and I ordered crawfish.

"Can we watch a movie while we eat?" Chris asked.

"If you say yes, I'll set up the TV trays and clean up afterwards."

For Chris and me, eating in the family room was a special treat. Dad had bought the TV trays because his family had them growing up, but Mom wasn't a fan. She wanted us to talk over dinner rather than watch TV. I was surprised when she shrugged and said, "Sure. Why not?"

I snuggled in with Charlie, trying to stay awake. I was still a bit tired and sore. I checked messages; Amie had responded.

Dear Kate,

I'm so sorry you had the flu and glad to hear you're on the mend. Take it easy, though, until you feel 100% better. Those of us with FOP have to be extra careful.

Once, after I had the flu, I had a flare-up in my forearm between my elbow and wrist. Since my left arm was already frozen straight, we put pillows under my right arm at night to keep it in a bent position. We wanted to make sure I had one arm that was positioned closer to my face so I'd still be able to feed myself.

FOP affects everyone differently, so I'm sure you'll be just fine, but to be on the safe side get plenty of rest.

Xoxo,

Amie

I hugged Charlie to stop feeling so anxious. It was a relief that what happened to Amie hadn't happened to me.

"Let's watch one of the *Star Wars* movies," Chris suggested.

I shook my head. I wasn't in the mood for shooting or any kind of battle. "I'd rather watch something really funny."

"Bueller!" Dad yelled, imitating the wacky school principal from *Ferris Bueller's Day Off*.

"Great idea," Chris agreed.

Ferris Bueller was a unanimous choice because we all loved him. He was the perfect character to make me forget that the flu and FOP even existed—at least for a while.

REMEMBER TO BREATHE

The next morning, I woke in terrible pain—a flare-up! It hurt to move my arms. I felt cold and numb, like the time Chris had thrown a bucket of water on my head during the Ice Bucket Challenge.

I rocked back and forth, softly moaning and crying for all the things I was afraid to lose. If my shoulders froze, I would need a *pick me stick* to raise my hand in class. I wouldn't be able to comb my hair without an extendable comb, or feed myself without tongs or a long-handled fork. But that wasn't even the worst of it. The worst was the fear. Worrying about what damage this flare-up might cause, when the next one might happen, where it would strike, and how much independence I would lose because of it. How could I live every single day with that much fear?

A deep hole opened inside of me. I fell in and couldn't climb out. Terrified, I reached for my phone on the bedside table and sent it clattering to the floor. I used a bad word, then scooched into a sitting position. I swung my legs over the side of the bed and squatted down. All that effort just to reach my phone.

I sent Amie a message. *Help me. I'm scared.*

Instead of messaging, Amie called right away. "Kate, what's wrong?!"

"I'm . . . I'm having a flare-up. My shoulders hurt. My arms hurt. And . . . and . . . I'm so scared."

"Of course you're scared," Amie said. Her voice was as soft and calm as mine was agitated. "I'm older than you are, and I've had lots more flare-ups. But I still get scared. Every. Single. Time."

"How do I live like this?" I wailed.

"Day by day. Try to stay in the moment and don't think the worst."

"Okay." My voice came out small and squeaky.

"I wish I was close enough to give you a hug," Amie said. "You did exactly the right thing by texting me. I always reach out to other people in the FOP community for advice. I've never run across a problem that somebody else hasn't had before me."

I sniffled, too choked up to answer.

"Let's take some deep breaths together," Amie said. "Sometimes the only way to keep from panicking is to remember you're not alone."

THE SECOND WEEK

During the second week of my flare-up, I was in too much pain to enjoy Thanksgiving—all I wanted to do was sleep. Mom worried over my loss of appetite, but nothing tasted good. She tried to tempt me with turkey, mashed potatoes, even gumbo. My stomach had forgotten how to be hungry.

Chris knocked on my door. "Kate, Mom had me collect all your assignments from school. You have a ton of homework."

"I'm tired. Leave it in the family room." My homework was piling up so fast, I'd never catch up, but I couldn't find the energy to really care.

Dad insisted I have dinner with the family. I sat at

the table, staring at my extendable fork and the long straw in my water glass. Mom had cut my pork tenderloin into tiny pieces. I was embarrassed. I didn't want to eat in front of anyone, not even Chris and my parents.

Mom got up from the table and disappeared into the kitchen. When she came back, she plopped a straw in everyone's water glass and handed Dad and Chris extendable forks. "The only way to get through this is together."

Chris waved his fork like an orchestra conductor. "What are we going to do about soup?"

I cracked a grin. "We'll get creative. Put it in a mug and sip it through a straw."

Mom laughed at Chris, who was still waving his fork. "That's what we've been missing around here—a sense of humor."

Mindy had sent more than fifty texts, but I hadn't answered any of them. It had been easier to ignore her. Now I punched her number into my phone, and she answered on the first ring. "I'm mad at you," she said.

"I figured you would be."

"Mateo's ghosting me too. He invited me to the fall dance, but I just want to be friends."

"Oh . . . I'm sorry about Mateo."

"I'm not nearly as upset about him as I am about you. Ghosting your best friend is unforgiveable."

I sucked in my breath. Unforgiveable was like FOP—permanent. "Min, I can't imagine how lonely I would be if you weren't still my best friend."

"You seem to be doing just fine without me."

"I'm not. Trust me." Since getting sick, I had done nothing but sleep to escape FOP. "The flu caused a flare-up and now my right arm is even worse than my left one. I've been having a hard time trying to accept it."

"I'm so sorry, but I bet . . . I bet . . ." I could tell by the way Mindy's voice broke that she had started to cry. "I bet you didn't ghost Amie."

"Amie's different. She's a grown-up and has flare-ups, like me."

Mindy didn't answer.

"Oh, Mindy, don't be mad. I need your help."

She sniffled. "Okay, but did you ever think sometimes I need a friend too? My dad called again. That's why I wanted to talk."

I felt lower than whale poop on the bottom of the ocean. "I messed up. How can I fix it?"

"You can stop keeping secrets and disappearing. I just need you to be honest with me."

"I promise."

"That's what you said the last time."

"I'll tell you a secret," I said. "Something I haven't even told Amie. When this flare-up started, it was like falling in a well. Remember when we watched that movie about the little girl who fell into the well?"

"Yes."

"I was in a dark place and I couldn't figure a way to climb out."

"Do you still feel that way?" Mindy asked.

"Sometimes."

"I think you should tell Amie or your mom. They'll know what to do."

The black hole terrified me. Before FOP, I'd never felt that way.

"How can I help?" Mindy asked. "I'd do anything to help you get well."

If only she could cure FOP, or even just stop it from getting worse. "I'm behind on my homework. Want to help me organize it this weekend? And then we can make Christmas cookies."

"Sounds like fun," Mindy said, "and we can start our Christmas movie marathon too. *Christmas on the Bayou* is playing on the Lifetime channel."

"Good. I don't think I've seen that one."

After Mindy and I hung up, I sat wrapped in memories of last Christmas. We had made reindeer-shaped cookies, watched movies, and gone to a live production of *The Nutcracker: A Tale from the Bayou*. I needed to remind Mom to buy our tickets for this year.

I thought some more about what Mindy had said. She was right. I reached for my phone and called Amie.

THE THIRD WEEK

I told Amie about falling in the black hole—how hopeless I'd been feeling.

"You might want to see a therapist," she said. "They can help you cope with your feelings, and it's nothing to be ashamed of. I saw one after the flare-up in my forearm."

"But my parents will be upset," I said.

"The reason they'll be upset is if you don't tell them how you're feeling."

Right away Mom got busy talking to my pediatrician and reading referrals.

From an old movie, I had a picture in my head of what a therapist should look like: an elderly, bearded gentleman in a suit. But Dr. Paula Stanley didn't look that way at all. She had short, wavy red hair, freckles, and wire-rimmed glasses, and she was wearing a blue button-down, chinos, and boat shoes.

I stared out the window at a crowded parking lot while Dr. Stanley talked to Mom and me about confidentiality. Basically, anything I said was between Dr. Stanley and me unless she was concerned that I might hurt myself or someone else. I wasn't worried about either of those things. I just wanted to feel good again.

After Mom left the room Dr. Stanley smiled and said, "Let's get to know each other. Tell me the story of Kate."

"I'm not used to talking to strangers, but my friend Amie says therapy helps."

"Your friend Amie is correct. Give me a chance, but if I'm not the right therapist for you, then your pediatrician can recommend others."

Dr. Stanley kept her eyes on my face and really listened to me. The black hole didn't seem to surprise her.

"What you're feeling is completely normal for someone who has been through a terrible trauma. Your nervous system has gone on high alert. I'll help you learn to calm it down."

"Amie says I have to remember to breathe."

Dr. Stanley nodded. "She's right again. We're going to train your breath, then I'll recommend a meditation app for your phone. I want you to spend ten minutes meditating first thing in the morning, ten minutes before you fall asleep, and ten minutes any time you feel extremely anxious. You can literally change your brain structure with a regular meditation practice."

"I've never meditated before."

"It takes practice, but it's really not that difficult. I'll guide you."

Dear Amie,

Thank you for recommending I see a therapist. I've only had one session, but it was a relief to hear that my feelings are normal. Dr. Stanley is teaching me to meditate. I'm not very good at it because my mind wanders, but Dr. Stanley says that's okay. She keeps repeating "return to the breath."

Xoxo,

Kate

Dear Kate,

Mindfulness is a great tool for everyone, but especially FOP patients. Before therapy, I spent too much time focusing on the future and worrying about things that may never happen, or obsessing about the past and thinking about things I couldn't change. My meditation mantra is day by day.

Xoxo,

Amie

I HOPE YOU DANCE

On Sunday afternoon, I was watching a Hallmark Christmas movie with Mom when I got a text from Izaak.

Beanie Weenie, you're lying down on the job. I need a math tutor.

I was nervous about Izaak noticing the way I'd lost movement in my arms. I used to compensate for my left arm with my right one, but that wasn't an option anymore.

"He's going to kiss her under the Christmas tree!" Mom said. "Why are you frowning?"

"A text from Izaak. He wants another tutoring session."

"So? Invite him over."

I pointed to my LSU T-shirt and cotton sleep pants. "I'd have to get dressed."

"Oh." Mom didn't say anything else, but the sad look in her eyes told me she'd understood. It was hard for me to change clothes. I had to use a dressing stick and it took forever.

"A dressing stick is like anything else," Mom said after a pause. "Learning to use it takes practice."

I rolled my eyes.

"It's true," Mom insisted.

Something inside me snapped. "Really? And how would *you* know?"

Mom's eyes got wide. They reminded me of a frightened deer I'd seen near Grandma and Grandpa's house.

I was breathing hard, like I'd just completed a tumbling run.

Finally, Mom said, "It's okay to be angry. If I had FOP, I would be angry too."

Angry didn't cover it. I was mad enough to burn the house down. We watched the rest of the stupid show in total silence.

Instead of starting another movie, Mom switched off the TV. "Want to talk about it?"

"No, there's nothing to say." Talking wouldn't help. I was sick of being miserable, and I realized Izaak always made me laugh. "I've changed my mind about calling Izaak."

Mom didn't comment. She was probably afraid of triggering another meltdown.

I stomped off to wrestle with the dressing stick, mumbling bad words under my breath.

"No cursing," Mom called.

I didn't care. If she had FOP, she would curse too.

While I got dressed, Mom had straightened up the family room and pulled two chairs in front of the table we used for board games. Chris was at choir practice for our church's Christmas pageant, so it was just Izaak and me. It was the first time I'd ever been alone with him.

Izaak pulled out his algebra book. "Word problems. The only thing worse than plain old X and Y equations is when you have to set them up for yourself."

I nudged him with my elbow. "You're not trying hard enough."

"That may be true," Izaak said, "but this algebra problem is dumb. Just listen to this: 'Justin is making a fort out of snowballs.' We live in Baton Rouge. No kids around here are making snowball forts."

The indignant look on his face cracked me up. I laughed harder than I'd laughed in weeks.

"You going to the Holly Dazzle dance?" Izaak asked.

I looked down at the floor, shaking my head.

"Why not?"

I wasn't sure how to answer him. The truth was that I couldn't raise my arms high enough to dance with any of the boys during slow songs, but I was too embarrassed to tell him.

"Come on, tell me. Why not?" Izaak repeated.

"You really want to know?"

"Yeah, that's why I asked."

I held both arms up. "This is as high as I can reach."

"Oh . . ." Izaak leaned back in his chair and squinted at me.

"Uh-oh. You're thinking again," I said.

Izaak tapped the side of his head with his index finger. "Shhh. Genius at work. I was remembering an old black-and-white movie I watched with my grandma. There's more than one way to dance."

"You mean like Fred Astaire and Ginger Rogers?"

"Not the tap-dancing stuff," Izaak said. "But you

191

could put your left arm around my waist, and then bend your right elbow so I could hold your hand." He wiggled his eyebrows.

It sounded wonderful, but Grandpa always said, *If something sounds too good to be true, it probably is.* "I bet you're asking because you feel sorry for me."

Izaak shook his head. "Bean, you got it all wrong. I'm asking because you're my friend and you laugh at my jokes."

That was the best answer in the world. Maybe Izaak really was a genius, just not at math. "All right. Okay, then. I'll go with you, but we have to practice dancing so the other kids won't stare."

Izaak pulled out his phone. "How about we watch some YouTube videos and see how it's done?"

As Izaak played "Slow Dancing in the Storm," my palms started to sweat. I put my left arm around his waist. My heart pounded.

"Relax, Beanie Weanie. Follow my lead."

I stepped on his foot. "Ouch," he yelped.

"Sorry!"

"That's okay. Not everybody is as light on their feet as me and Fred Astaire."

I laughed—it was impossible not to.

Izaak and I didn't make much progress with word problems, but we got pretty good at dancing together.

Sometimes Mom quotes this author Glennon Doyle, who says, "We can do hard things." Getting dressed had been hard, but twirling around the floor with Izaak had definitely been worth it.

LETTING GO

"**H**ow are you feeling about going back to school tomorrow?" Dr. Stanley asked at our next session.

"Nervous. I think I'm going to have lunch in the library. I'm not ready for kids to stare at me while I eat a sandwich with tongs."

Dr. Stanley pulled off her glasses and wiped them with a cleaning cloth. "Have you considered telling some of your friends about the tongs? I bet they'd be sympathetic."

"Probably, but that still wouldn't keep other kids from staring."

"Those kids are just curious," Dr. Stanley said. "They've never seen anyone eat a sandwich with tongs before, so they're searching for an explanation. Once they have one, they'll go back to minding their own business."

I sighed. "Maybe, but I hate being different."

"How has the meditation app been working?"

"I like it. I really like it. It's easy to use, and the monk's voice is so soothing. I relax as soon as he starts to talk."

Dr. Stanley smiled. "Good. That's the whole idea. Now let's discuss fear. Tell me what you're most afraid of."

I leaned back against the leather sofa and stared at the walls decorated with paintings of sailboats. I wondered what it would be like to sail on one of them. "That's easy. Another flare-up."

"Whenever you're afraid of the future, I want you to focus on the present. Pay attention to what you can see, hear, smell, and touch. Let's try it right now. What do you see?"

"Pictures of sailboats. Are you a sailor?"

She nodded. "Yes. Yes, I am. What do you hear?"

"Muffled voices. Probably the receptionist."

"What about smell?"

I closed my eyes and inhaled. "Mint tea."

"Very good. I had a cup just before our session started. What about touch?"

"The leather couch."

"You have no control over the thing you're most afraid of," Dr. Stanley said. "So, if you accept that and stay in the present, you'll spend less time being afraid. Does that make sense?"

"Yes." I squeezed my eyes shut tighter and focused on taking belly breaths.

"You're trying to control something you never had control of in the first place," Dr. Stanley said. "Accept it, and let the fear go."

I was afraid to let go.

"You never had control in the first place," Dr. Stanley repeated.

Never had control.

Never had control.

Never had control.

Ever since my diagnosis, a hard knot had formed inside my chest. I pictured it as a stone with sharp edges. I focused on the stone, willing it to crumble. I breathed into that space until my chest felt loose, like I'd stretched a muscle that had been pulled too tight.

Admitting I had no control over FOP was astounding. I had spent weeks resisting, trying to change something that couldn't be changed.

Now, for a moment, I felt free.

THE DREADED TONGS

I stood in the school hallway with my insulated bag, trying to decide whether to eat in the library or brave the lunchroom. I had followed through on one of the things Dr. Stanley had suggested. I'd sent Jayla a text explaining how I had to use tongs. *No worries,* she had responded. But Jayla was my friend. A lot of the kids who would be staring didn't really know me.

In the library, Ms. Batiste was working on the computer. She looked up. "Nice to see you, Kate."

I pulled out my sandwich and the dreaded tongs. I really didn't have much appetite.

"How about a brownie?" Ms. Batiste asked. "I baked some last night."

I ate my lunch backward. The brownie first and then half of the sandwich.

"Having a hard first day back?"

I remembered some of the tips from Dr. Stanley and tried to relax my jaw and shoulders. Deep breaths helped too. "I keep noticing all the things other kids can do that I can't."

"Comparison is the thief of joy," Ms. Batiste said. "Theodore Roosevelt said that. Instead of worrying about all the things you can't do, you should focus on the things you *can* still do. Make a list and write them down."

I nodded. "That sounds like something my therapist, Dr. Stanley, would say."

Ms. Batiste laughed. "Some days I don't think there's much difference between being a librarian and being a therapist."

While I was wiping up crumbs, Jayla pulled open the door to the library and plopped down in front of me. "Thought I'd find you here."

"I was too self-conscious to eat in front of everyone."

Jayla slid an envelope across the table. "It's an invitation to my birthday party. We're going to the movies and then we'll have cake and ice cream."

I used to love going to the movies, but not anymore.

It would embarrass me to eat popcorn with a fork. "Who's going to be there?"

"I've invited you, Claire, Nat, Harper, and my cousins, Jesmyn and Stephanie. You'll really like my cousins."

"I'm not sure I can make it."

The smile slid from Jayla's face. "What do you mean you can't make it? You haven't even opened the invitation to check the date."

I held up the tongs. "I can't reach to eat popcorn, so I'd either have to use these or an extendable fork. Can you imagine the strange looks I'd get from the other girls?"

Jayla shrugged in an effortless way I couldn't manage anymore because of the tightness in my shoulders.

Comparison is the thief of joy.

"A fork won't bother Stephanie at all," Jayla said. "When her brother was going through chemo, she shaved her head to support him and didn't care who stared at her."

"If she *really* didn't care, then she's braver than I am. I'd like to meet her."

"Then come to my party," Jayla said. "No excuses."

INTO THE UNKNOWN

Mom dropped me off in front of the mall. I hummed along to "Silent Night," enjoying the Christmas trees, wreaths, and lights. I was looking forward to the movie, a fantasy, with flying dragons.

Claire, Nat, and Harper stood near the entrance to the theater. "Hey, Kate!"

Jayla tapped me on the shoulder. "I want you to meet my cousins, Jesmyn and Stephanie."

Jesmyn looked like Jayla. They had the same dark skin and high cheekbones. Stephanie had white skin, but when I looked closer, I saw that she had the same cheekbones too.

Claire and Harper had both worn black leggings

with matching Uggs. Last year, it would have been Claire and me who had dressed alike. I wished Mindy had been invited. She had been so excited when I told her that I'd danced with Izaak.

Mrs. Jackson bought our tickets, then ordered soda and popcorn for everyone. I had brought my own straw. Mom had insisted on the extendable fork, but there was no way I'd actually use it. I'd say I wasn't hungry and offer my popcorn to the other girls.

I took the aisle seat, waiting for the movie to start. Stephanie sat on the other side of me, munching popcorn. It was so easy for her to dip her fingers inside the bag and raise them to her lips.

Comparison is the thief of joy.

"I asked Jayla if I could sit beside you," Stephanie said. She had a friendly smile and her green eyes sparkled.

"Really? I wanted to meet you too."

"Jayla told me you gave an awesome speech in front of your entire school. I'd like to do something like that at my school to help raise money for Rhabdomyosarcoma."

"What's that?" I asked.

"A rare childhood cancer that my brother has." She stopped munching on popcorn long enough to point at her short hair. "I shaved off my hair when Michael lost his from chemo. It's just now starting to grow back."

"I bet the other kids stared at you."

Stephanie shrugged. "Some did, but that was their problem, not mine."

I glared at the bag of popcorn in my lap; my stomach growled from its buttery smell. FOP had taken so many things away from me, but giving up popcorn was *my* choice. I thought of Izaak and remembered dancing with him. I had almost let FOP take that away from me too.

"So, do you have any public speaking tips for me?" Stephanie asked.

I reached into my jacket pocket and touched the extendable fork. Was I brave enough to use it? "Smile and speak slowly," I said.

Coming attractions scrolled across the movie screen, but I didn't pay much attention. I kept rubbing my fingers across the fork handle.

The movie finally started, but I couldn't concentrate on it. I thought of Ms. Batiste saying I should focus on the things I can still do. I could still eat popcorn.

The heroine embarked on a quest to save her kingdom. Guided by a wizard, she entered the petrified forest. I admired her bravery, but Freya didn't have to face her problems alone. She had her friends, an ogre and a flying dragon.

As Freya journeyed into the petrified forest, I thought about my own personal quest. FOP had presented so many obstacles, like giving up gymnastics and having to use a dressing stick. I rubbed the extendable fork handle. This wasn't just about popcorn, but about my future. Did I have the courage to be like Freya and journey into the unknown? Was I brave enough to do all sorts of things differently from other kids, even if they stared? I rubbed the fork handle so hard, it must have been magic or else it would have snapped. I didn't have to let FOP win.

I looked past Stephanie at the other girls, silently saying their names: *Claire, Harper, Jayla, Nat, and Jesmyn.* Would I embarrass them? Did it really matter?

I pulled the fork out of my pocket and extended it as far as it would reach. Stephanie turned her head and smiled as I speared three fluffy pieces of popcorn. It was the most delicious thing I had ever tasted.

THE KEY TO HAPPINESS

After finding a pattern, Mom had whipped out her sewing machine and made my dress for the dance out of red brocade. Like Amie's wedding gown, it was in two pieces, with a covered zipper, so I wouldn't have to raise my arms overhead to put it on.

I checked my appearance in the full-length mirror that still had a crack in it. My hair hung in loose curls and I'd used just a touch of blush and lip gloss. I felt beautiful.

The dress suited me, but I couldn't decide if it needed a necklace. I rummaged through my jewelry box, but nothing seemed just right. I sat down on my bed, careful not to wrinkle my dress, and thought of everything that had happened in the last couple of weeks.

I had started managing the gymnastics team. The job was easy, but it took a lot of time to make sure all permission slips were signed and that each girl's medical history and insurance information was up-to-date. My favorite part of being manager, though, was cheering for my friends. Claire had nailed her bars routine and won the all-around gold medal, and I had honestly been happy for her, yet a little sad for myself too. Not that long ago, I had won my own gold medal. When Claire hopped off the podium she had sprinted over to me and hung her medal around my neck. "You're still a champion," she whispered. "Braver than I could ever be."

Claire had totally surprised me. I'd invited Jayla to go swimming and I had reached out to Nat about a Field Day for FOP, but I had never reached out to Claire. And then . . . wow.

Thinking back, I wasn't sure that what Claire whispered was entirely true. It wasn't that I was braver than other kids. I just hadn't been given much choice—it was either find a way to be happy or stay miserable. Claire's medal was lying on my dresser—a reminder not to judge my friends too harshly.

I looked away from my reflection and over to the poster of Freya that had replaced the shadow of Aly Raisman. I needed one more poster and this one should come from my heart. I sat down and wrote a poem—a reminder of the girl I was, and the young woman I hoped to become.

I Can

I can watch the sunrise.
I can smell bacon cooking.
I can eat pancakes and eggs.
I can study the earth, and moon, and stars.
I can imagine castles, and dungeons, and dragons.
I can follow recipes and bake cookies.
I can get slobbery kisses from my dog.
I can be a math tutor.
I can sing along to musicals.
I can dance with Izaak.
I can write a speech.
I can speak before a crowd.
I can raise money for research.
I can ask my friends for help.

I read through the poem. It held the key to being happy: focusing on the things I could still do.

"Bean," Mom called. "Izaak's here."

I put down my pen, took one last look in the mirror, and went to join him.

"That's some dress," Izaak said. "Red is my favorite color."

Happiness bubbled up inside me, the stars were shining through our picture window, and I couldn't wait to dance.

A NOTE FROM AUTHOR
AMIE DARNELL SPECHT

I was born with the genetic condition Fibrodysplasia Ossificans Progressiva, or FOP, and it became active when I was four years old due to immunizations into my thigh muscle. Any type of trauma, whether it be stress or physical, can cause FOP to erupt.

FOP is extremely rare. It's estimated to affect about 3,500 people worldwide. It is caused by a gene mutation or is passed on by a parent who has FOP. No one else in my family has the condition.

I attended public schools and was in regular and gifted classes. I ended up graduating high school at the age of sixteen, with my brother, Kurt, who was seventeen. I used a walker as a child, then around thirteen started using a manual wheelchair instead of a walker. At seventeen after a major flare-up due to the flu, I lost some mobility and by twenty-five was using a power chair full-time.

My parents very much wanted me to experience life. I would climb trees and ride four-wheelers. My childhood was as typical as I could manage, because we all knew that one day I would not be able to live a typical life. In high school I did a lot of public speaking, including to the entire school (around 2,000 people), the Lions Club, and the school board. I was involved in activities in high school as well: choir, student council, Girl Scouts, theater arts, and religious education.

Gymnastics, however, was the activity most important to me, and I became the manager of the team. My speech to the school board was an effort to save the gymnastics team because the board was considering cutting the program and I wanted them to know how much it meant to me.

In 2007, I got married. My husband, Matt, and I live in our own house with four pets. At first, I could do everything for myself, but as my disease has progressed, Matt has become my caregiver.

When Shannon and I wrote *Dancing in the Storm*, there was no treatment available for FOP, but on August 16, 2023, the U.S. FDA approved a drug called Sohonos (palovarotene). We hope this treatment, along with more in the years to come, will help improve the quality of life for FOP patients.

I am thrilled to be able to share my story so that readers will understand what a person with a disability faces, and that we go through the same emotions as everyone else. My thanks to my friend and co-author, Shannon Hitchcock, who suggested that we write this book.

A NOTE FROM AUTHOR SHANNON HITCHCOCK

I first heard about Fibrodysplasia Ossificans Progressiva on my neighbor Tammara Darnell's Facebook page. I knew Tammara had an adult daughter who used a wheelchair, but I had never asked why, because I didn't want to appear nosy or rude.

Later that day, I googled FOP and was intrigued by what I read. The official IFOPA website defines the disorder this way: "One of the rarest, most disabling conditions known to medicine, FOP causes bone to form in muscles, tendons, ligaments, and other connective tissues. Bridges of extra bone develop across joints, progressively restricting movement and forming a second skeleton that imprisons the body in bone.

There are no other known examples in medicine of one normal organ system turning into another."

As often happens, what I read made my heart feel heavy, and I remembered this quote by Isak Dinesen: "All sorrows can be borne if you put them into a story or tell a story about them." I called my neighbor and asked if she thought her daughter, Amie, would be interested in writing a book with me. Amie graciously said yes.

In the winter of 2020, Amie and I started meeting at the home she shares with her husband, Matt. Amie told me stories of her childhood and candidly discussed living with FOP. All was going according to plan until COVID-19 struck. Individuals living with FOP are at a higher risk of complications like pneumonia, and so my sessions with Amie evolved into private messages and e-mail exchanges. We developed a rhythm. Amie would tell me a story, I'd write it down, and then she would review what I'd written and suggest changes.

One of my most exhilarating moments in writing this book was speaking with Dr. Fred Kaplan, who is the Isaac and Rose Nassau Professor of Orthopaedic Molecular Medicine at the University of Pennsylvania School of Medicine. Dr. Fred, as he is affectionately known by his patients, has dedicated his life to unraveling the mysteries of FOP.

My hope in collaborating with Amie is to draw attention to this crippling disease, inspire fundraising for research, and promote empathy for people living with disabilities. For more information, visit: https://www.ifopa.org/ and read *Finding Magic Mountain* by Carol Zapata-Whelan.

ACKNOWLEDGMENTS

Although our names are on the cover, this novel required a team to become a reality. We would especially like to thank Dr. Fred Kaplan for answering Shannon's questions about diagnosing FOP, Dr. Tori Leigh Kelley for lending her expertise regarding Kate's meditation practice, and Kimberly Vidal for helping with the gymnastics routines. The following writers served as early readers: Nancy Stewart, Sue LaNeve, Augusta Scattergood, and Lorin Oberweger. We also owe a huge debt of gratitude to FOP mom and fellow author, Carol Zapata-Whelan, who served as a sensitivity reader.

And finally, much love to our agent, Deborah Warren, who made the connection with Lauri Hornik, the perfect editor for this story.